OUR
SIMPLE
GIFTS

ALSO BY OWEN PARRY

Honor's Kingdom

Call Each River Jordan

Shadows of Glory

Faded Coat of Blue

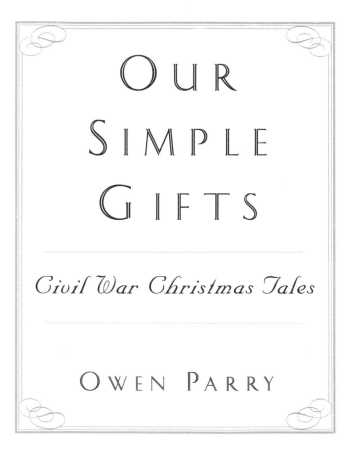

OUR SIMPLE GIFTS

Civil War Christmas Tales

OWEN PARRY

wm

WILLIAM MORROW

An Imprint of HarperCollins*Publishers*

HarperCollins books may be purchased for educational, business, or sales promotional use. For information please write: Special Markets Department, HarperCollins Publishers Inc., 10 East 53rd Street, New York, NY 10022.

FIRST EDITION

Designed by Jo Anne Metsch

Printed on acid-free paper

Library of Congress Cataloging-in-Publication Data

Parry, Owen.
Our simple gifts : Civil War Christmas tales / by Owen Parry.—1st ed.
p. cm.
ISBN 0-06-001378-8
1. United States—History—Civil War, 1861–1865—Fiction.
2. Christmas stories, American 3. War stories, American. I. Title.
PS3566.A7637 O97 2002
813'.54—dc21   2002068480

02 03 04 05 06 JTC/QW 10 9 8 7 6 5 4 3 2 1

To my father,
who loved Christmas

Contents

OUR SIMPLE GIFTS

Star of Wonder

HE SNOW CHARGED out of the dusk and surrounded the train. Beyond the flake-shot glass, the dark hills paled. Captured, the fields lay under flags of surrender. The locomotive fought on and the file of cars shivered and clattered over a bridge. Beyond a lifeless canal, ice crept out from the black banks of the river. Although he sat only one bench from the coal stove at the head of the aisle, Robert gathered the blue greatcoat over his chest with the hand the war had left him.

He understood the cold as soldiers do, and felt it waiting in ambush.

The whistle shrieked to warn a town of the train's approach. Lighted windows flashed by, yellow and beckoning, past swirling veils of snow. One rectangle framed a German tree and Robert caught a glimpse of dancing figures. As the engine slowed, brakes keened and billows of steam thickened the snow until Robert could not see the outside world at all.

When the car stopped, big Dutchmen lugged their parcels toward the door. The nailheads on their soles scraped the coal grit deeper into the planks. The sound was instantly familiar to Robert. The miners swore the coal got into their blood until it darkened the color. It certainly got into the floor of any wagon that made the run between Reading and Pottsville.

The grinding of those boots was his first welcome.

A doll's head peeped from a traveler's sack. Delayed for a moment at the threshold of the car, the last of the Dutchmen looked back to where Robert sat, glanced over his uniform, and said, *"Frohe Weihnachten, Herr Hauptmann. Alles gute."*

"Merry Christmas," Robert answered, in a voice colder than he had intended.

"And what's a Christmas Eve, would you tell us that, then, without a proper bit o' celebration?" a grinning new passenger demanded. He dropped onto the bench opposite Robert, cocked an eyebrow under a snow-dappled Derby hat he did not remove, and made a great show of looking up and down the car, although there was little enough for anyone to see. Wise men and the fortunate had been at home for hours, or in church or chapel for the early service. Surrounded by those they loved.

"Is there a happy thirst yet in ye, Captain, sir?" The fellow held out an unstoppered bottle of whisky in a hand raw as a field surgeon's. "Have ye a thirst that wants a quenching this fine and blessed eve?" Then his eyes found the empty sleeve, lifted at once to Robert's face and settled on the lamp behind his shoulder. The Irishman held the bottle out another inch. "There's more good in it than harm, say as they mought, and the broth from the bottle's a comfort."

The Irishman wore a patched brown overcoat with caped shoulders that once had belonged to a gentleman. The snow that dressed it had already melted on the side toward the stove, leaving it mottled with patches of wet. A home-knit scarf coiled around the man's neck like a snake. His shoes would not have lasted a good day's march.

Robert attempted a smile and waved the bottle away. "I haven't the constitution for it," he lied. The last time he had tasted whisky he had tasted a great deal too much of it. That had been at summer's end, after the letter came. The letter had seemed a horrible joke, penned in the midst of a war, its news wrong and impossible. He had read it again and again, reading as he drank, and the whisky was already behind him when next the dull edge of his saber settled back against his shoulder and he repeated the colonel's commands in his practiced voice to set his shrunken company marching toward a hostile line of rifles. The whisky had been behind him then, but not the letter, and he had gone into his last battle in the grip of a selfish madness.

Now he was going home.

The Irishman sighed and the train groaned back into motion, dusting off the snow that had frosted the windows during the stop.

"I'm ever a steady man meself, when there's work that wants a doing," the little fellow said. "But an't it Christmas come round again, and here's to the joy and the blessings." He hoisted the bottle near to his lips, then paused at the instant of drinking. "Sure, and ye don't mind if I take a quick drop meself, Captain, sir? Ye'll not take offense, high gentleman that ye are?"

Robert shook his head. Chased by the onslaught of snow, the locomotive throbbed up the valley toward the end of the line.

"Is it home ye're off to, then, sir? Is that where ye're all about going this blessed eve?"

"Yes." He had not written, and they did not expect him. He wanted to surprise them, to see that much brief happiness on the faces of his mother and father, his sister. He had thought about that moment of homecoming so often during his journey northward that he had become greedy for it. He longed for joy, even if it belonged to others and was no more than a reflected happiness. And now it was as if he had written and promised them, as if he were expected, after all, and must not disappoint. It was unreasonable, of course, just another form of the madness that had come over him, the rage at life that no one else could see. But there was nothing more important in the world now than his arrival at home for Christmas day. "Yes, I'm going home."

"Well, here's to the joy o' that, too. For there's no place like home, and there's no disputing the matter. Ah, the war's a terrible thing in all its black doings, taking the boys from home, and some forever." The fellow swigged from his bottle and finished with a smack. "Oh, don't I wish every one o' the lads was home by his hearth for Christmas? I could weep for the thought o' their loneliness down in Virginny."

Robert wondered what this man in cast-off clothes knew about loneliness. A great deal, perhaps. Perhaps that was the one thing everyone learned about. For Charlotte to die at home, in comfort and what had seemed impregnable safety . . . where was the sense in that? Where was the great cause? The meaning? Of a fever, they said. Typhoid fever. He had wanted to marry before he left, but Charlotte insisted on waiting, as did their families, no matter their satisfaction at the match. "One must not be precipitous," his father had counseled. "These things must be done properly, war or no war." And now she was dead. Death was precipitous, whether men were or not.

"Ah, but it's young ye are, Captain, sir," the Irishman said, as if peering into Robert's thoughts. "Young and flush with the sap o' life." He glanced again at the overcoat's empty sleeve. "And little tribulations will not stop ye, for they're given to us in Grace to be overcome." Settling back on the bench, he stared at his near-empty bottle, then grew earnest. "And when will we all be shut o' this wicked war? Can ye only tell us that, sir? When mought we have the boys back down the pits and out o' this bloody Virginny? When will we all be shut o' the thing, can ye give us so much as a hint?"

"I'm shut of it," Robert said, then regretted his words. They were shameful and unmanly. And, he realized, they were absolutely honest.

"And cheap at the cost, if ye want me own opinion. For many's the lad what will never come home at all."

Not a mile short of Pottsville, the conductor stepped into the car. The Irishman made the bottle disappear and seemed to drop off into slumber as if it were death.

The conductor kicked him. "You again, McArdle? I don't suppose you have a ticket this time, either?"

"He's my guest," Robert said quickly. "Just a moment." He began undoing his overcoat's buttons to get to his purse. He had learned to be almost dexterous in three months, yet one hand would never be as good as two.

The conductor looked him over in the order that Robert had learned to predict: a brief reading of the face, next of his rank, then the uniform as a whole, climaxing at the empty sleeve. Then the eyes returned to Robert's face for an instant before looking away.

"Never mind, sir," the conductor said. "We'll mark it down to Christmas, and none's the wiser. The line's apologies again for the want of a decent car, sir, but the gentry all come up on the morning train." Before continuing down the aisle, he gave the Irishman a milder tap with the toe of his boot. "Christmas comes but once a year, McArdle. And you'll do yourself a favor to remember it."

"A happy Christmas and a merry one to you, sir," the Irishman replied. His eyes shone with the delight of a bad child who had gotten away with a prank.

When the conductor had gone and with the train already slowing, the Irishman leaned toward Robert and said, "Herod Antipas himself wan't half so hard as the sort what gets work on the railways. Little tin gods every one o' them, and no use to any at all."

Metal skated over wet metal and the car rolled into clouds of steam again. The snow had grown so heavy that Robert could not see the lights of the town he knew must be there.

"But ye, sir," the Irishman went on. "Oh, it's a proper gentleman ye are, and I knew it before ever I set me down. For I'll not consort with the bad trade, not Billy McArdle. Trouble's contagious as plague and ye never—"

"Are you married?" Robert asked suddenly.

"Me? And don't I look like a normal fool of a man to ye, and in me years o' propriety? And show me the man o' propriety what an't made the grand mistake. Oh, I'm married up and down, 'tis married I am, and all blessed by the Holy Mother Church." He sighed. "Truth be told, the old girl's not the worst o' them. There'll be a lovely supper in the pot, though she'll drag me off to mass for the price o' the tasting."

"Children?"

"Five. Though it mought have been seven, had the measles not come upon us." The Irishman put on a quizzical look, as if unused to questions of such a nature.

The conductor came back through, calling, "Pottsville, last stop, Pottsville . . ." But Robert barely heard him, or recognized the Irishman any longer. Only the memory of Charlotte was real, and the thought of children never to be born. It was all such idiocy. They all believed it was the loss of his arm that had left his spirits as black as his beard, but the arm was little enough. Other men had lost far more. Much, much more. "One must not be precipitous," his father had said. And now he would never see her again, nor feel her beside him or touch her. Life went on, but he did not go with it.

"Are ye feeling a bit queer, then, Captain, sir?" the Irishman asked him. The fellow stood, though not steadily. Another passenger nearly toppled him in pushing toward the door. "Is it a fever come upon ye, or somewhat else o' the like?"

"I'm fine," Robert said, rising himself. On his feet, he stood more than a head taller than the Irishman.

Robert reached for his bag and the Irishman made to go.

But at the step, the little man turned and said, "Merry Christmas, sir. And may the blessings o' the day fall heavy upon ye."

"Merry Christmas," Robert answered dully.

HASTE CONFOUNDED THE crowd upon the platform. Those too anxious to flee the cold slipped on new ice and fell, and slush licked over boot-tops as the windward side of overcoats gathered the snow. Voices cried out names and greetings, while others offered cab rides at fair rates or warned the railway navvies to have a care as leather trunks came flying from the baggage car. Bells pealed in the distance, and children ran amok.

As he stepped down and let go of the help-rail, Robert saw a soldier descending from the next wagon back. The man wore an enlisted soldier's plain cap and braced himself on crutches as he struggled down the steps of the car. One pant leg was pinned up. The cloth dangled like an empty sling just below the hem of the soldier's overcoat.

The hands of strangers reached out to help the boy down, and then a woman's voice pierced the hubbub of the crowd, more powerful than the last letting off of steam, cancelling the nickering and the impatient hooves of horses, and vanquishing even the sound of the Christmas bells.

"*Jimmy!*" she cried, and she ran for him, shawl blazing out

behind her as she slipped but did not fall and thrust herself between the bulk of strangers.

The leg-lost boy alerted, and Robert saw a look of flawless
wonder come over his face. Then the woman, hardly more
than a girl, had her arms about him, hugging, clutching, cling-
ing, and burying her face so tightly against the bosom of his
coat that the boy almost toppled backward. Nor would she let
go, or speak, or even open her eyes, as if afraid all this might
be a dream.

Such a public display would have been unthinkable before
the war changed all of them. But now those lingering about
the platform broke into applause and hurrahs, and cries of
"Merry Christmas" filled the air. Robert spotted one middle-
aged man dabbing his eyes with a handkerchief.

But this show of happiness was only another blow to Robert,
and he felt himself grow small with jealousy, for he knew that
no one in the world would cling to him like that now.

The crowd dissolved, driven homeward by the storm. As
the platform cleared, Robert saw that a startling depth of
snow had already piled up where no one trod, and the rough
street between the station and the first blurred lights of the
town was fast becoming a canyon walled by snow.

He found his trunk and had a porter bring it along. In hope
of a fattened tip, the fellow complained of the cold and the
need to work on Christmas Eve for his family's sake. Robert
resented the man's shamelessness, but would not disappoint

him, since he always prided himself on being a more generous man with servants than his father could bring himself to be. It had been their only point of disagreement, until the matter of a wedding date was broached.

No, we must not be precipitous.

Robert swore to himself that every fool should be damned to Hell who did not grasp at happiness the instant it was offered.

Charlotte.

He had difficulty hiring a rig for the last dozen miles of his journey. The cab-men all agreed that the snow confined their traps to the streets and lanes of the town, and even the shabbiest pony-cart driver would not risk the trip over the hill to Saint Clair, let alone the hard stretch over the mountain beyond. Robert's desperation boiled until his temper threatened all the world around him, a quality he never had displayed in his life before. Not even when men died around him, nor when they took his arm. Not even Charlotte's death had brought him to a temper. To a closed, private madness, perhaps. Even unto despair. But not to anger at his fellow man.

He approached the second-to-last rig in the dwindling line, with the porter whining and worrying behind him. A quick, little fellow with a narrow face had swapped his pony cart for an ancient black sleigh drawn by a shaggy mare.

When Robert put his request, the driver merely turned his

face to the sky. The big, fast snowflakes wet his face and made him blink.

"Hard weather, see," the driver said, Welsh as salt cod and chapels. "I do not know that Sweetie will do for the mountain, sir, for she's not the youngest in the stable, that she is not. Look you. I will take you in the morning, with a proper pair in the harness, if you have a mind to wait the night."

Robert struggled to master himself. While the properly brought-up, educated man he revealed to the world understood the sense of the driver's counsel, the demon newly released wanted to strike out, to resolve the matter with blows against man and horse. He *had* to reach home. By morning. To see his mother's face, her transient fear rushing into joy, and his father's crumbling reserve, and the brightness in the eyes of his sister, Amelia. There was no choice, not of the sort that men imagine for themselves. He was bound to go on, no matter the price in money, flesh or pain.

"I need to go on tonight," Robert said in a voice so calm it amazed him.

"Well . . . I will tell you, then. As it is Christmas Eve, I will take you as far as Saint Clair, though the fare must be doubled, for all my risk and troubles. And when we get to Saint Clair, we will see how the weather lies, and then we will make our judgement. But double the fare it is, and I will have no bargaining."

"I'll triple it," Robert said. Quickly, as if afraid the man might change his mind, he told the porter to put up his trunk. And when the man moved too slowly for him, Robert tossed his bag on the seat and added a third arm to the effort.

On the hillside that butted down against the main street, a brace of mansions glowed. A small orchestra sounded from one of the parlors, ending a *Schottische* then starting up a polka, and Robert heard the silver ring of laughter. There would be punch, and pale shoulders, and thoughtless gaiety. He knew he might have found a welcome and a bed at any of a dozen good houses, but their joys were not his and his homeward journey had become as fixed before him as an invisible star. Had he not been raised to believe in a man's free will, he would have said this journey was his destiny. But he was tired and worn, and he knew his judgement in such matters must not be trusted.

They crossed through the middle of the town, where fading revelers battled the snow and the church bells seemed to beg for guests at the altar. A band of carolers, likely Welsh themselves, roamed through the streets, but the storm had dampened their custom. Still, their voices promised and soothed, singing of angels on high. And where the shuttered shops declined in quality, bright-lit saloons spilled men into the street and festive songs came rollicking, heedless and out of tune. A ragged woman scolded as she helped a man stagger home. He cursed a distant queen and fell in a snowdrift.

"They will drink themselves sorry," the driver called back

over his shoulder, "and have no joy of the day come Christmas morn. A man should be home this night, if not required to do his honest labor. But they are Irish, see, and blinded by Rome."

Yes, the Irish. Robert had shared the attitudes of his class and kind before the war, not least the notion that all of the Irish were children and needful of strictness. Then he had seen them fight as well as any, and learned enough of the pit-head lads in his company to suspect they were the same as other men, if benighted of intellect. Some drank too much, but so did many others. Some ran away, but cowards came in every kind, and a childhood friend of his who had become a major through pull disgraced himself by hiding up a tree. And McLeod had been the son of a wealthy family. The Irish were . . . troubling. But their humanity could not be denied.

You learned things in a war. You learned them, but that did not mean you understood them at once. Robert sensed that he would struggle through the business of understanding what he had seen and done and felt for many years to come, if those years were granted him.

The sleigh pulled out of the clutter of shanties and stables that bothered the end of the town and the mare climbed the winding road that crossed the ridge. The single lantern swinging by the driver's side was soon the only light in the world, and the snowflakes struck its glass like a torrent of moths. The course turned them into the full of the wind, and the snow had the weight of dust kicked up by a regiment of cavalry, then more weight still, and Robert coaxed his collar higher and tipped down his hat, dropping snow into his lap. He swept his beard until it was largely black again, but the snow rushed back in moments. His fine calf glove was already wet through. Up on his bench, the driver made himself as small as he could and Robert felt the straining of the horse.

No other vehicle had chosen to brave the road, and the driver complained that he could not see the way. They slithered and skated as the road led downward again, and twice they nearly spilled into a ditch. But the Welshman knew his craft and got them down, though they had to come within fifty yards of the first houses before Robert could make out the least light from the town.

The heavy snow turned finer and sharper until it cut the skin with the force of a whip. The night sizzled.

A chapel emptied on a corner and huddled figures hurried through the blow. The town seemed eerily quiet, with many a house closed snug against the storm, tamping the light given off by the lamps within. Golden blades cut across the snow where shutters did not quite meet and fanlights glowed above the front doors of foremen and counting-house clerks.

Past the watchman's lantern by the colliery gates, a black wall rose up behind the maelstrom of white.

The driver pulled back on the reins. Clutched by a drift, the sleigh came to a halt.

"Well," the Welshman said, twisting and leaning back to be heard by his passenger, "I have done as I have promised. But look you and you will see. There is no going farther, for the snow is come up to her belly and I will be a lucky man if I see my home tonight."

"I'll pay you twenty dollars," Robert called.

The Welshman hesitated. He was frosted over with snow. Then he shook his head. "A life is worth more, see. At least mine is to me, I cannot say for others. And any man who would go over the mountain in such a storm is a fool. Begging your pardon, sir."

"*Fifty* dollars."

The driver shook his head vehemently, though his snow-crusted brow wrinkled to express a mixture of greed and sympathy. "It is not the money, see. Though glad enough I would be of it, sir. But we would not go far, though far enough it might be to see us frozen and dead as Prince Albert. And if we did not die, the horse would, surely. Look you. What good would that be to any man?"

Robert's temper had quieted under the assault of the storm, but his resolve was undiminished. If anything, it had grown stronger as he felt himself coming closer to home with each mile, with each next step of the horse. He paid the driver, generously, and told him where to send his trunk the next day.

"Do you understand?" Robert asked, nearly shouting to be heard against the howl of the wind.

The driver nodded solemnly. "I do, sir."

"Good. Send it along as early as you can."

"Sir? You'll not go on, will you? Afoot like?"

"Yes. I'm going on."

The driver shook his head so broadly the snow tumbled from his shoulders. "God bless you, sir, you're taking your own life."

Robert almost made an angry boast that nothing was going to stop him, but paused just short of taunting God and man.

"I'm used to marching," was all he said, and he turned into the wind.

He did not look back. Just as he had never looked back in battle because he did not want his men to see the terror on his face, nor did he want them to think he doubted them and feared they would not follow. And so many had followed him and died, imagining that he knew best because he came from a better class and wore a captain's rank he had not earned. Often, he had worried that he was a coward, but somehow he always managed to put one foot in front of the other until the battle gripped and possessed him, and all thought fled, and the demonic rapture told him what to do and he did it.

So Robert did not look backward now, but he knew the driver was watching him go, not only because the whip did not snap and the sleigh did not creak with the horse struggling to turn it. He knew it in the depths of his belly, just as he knew that a moment would come when his figure became small unto vanishing, and the spell would be broken, and the Welshman would turn homeward.

The going was hard from the first. Within fifteen minutes, he regretted that he had not left his satchel bag behind with the trunk. He was still thinking as a man with two arms and two hands thought. And it was hard to nudge a drooping scarf back over the ears or to catch a hat about to blow away, to brush off a weight of snow from chest and shoulders and close a collar again with a lone hand burdened with a bag.

And it was the queerest thing. His missing arm felt colder than the arm of flesh and blood. He often had sensations of the sort, a baffling business. But now the chill in the ghostly limb was positively painful. As if it were bared to the night.

In half an hour, he was soaked with sweat and breathing with difficulty.

He was a fool. In a thousand ways. Of course, the driver had been right. But Robert was sick to death with doing things properly, and with men who always knew what was right and sensible. "One must not be precipitous." Did precipitous mean you were about to leap off a precipice? Then he longed to jump. "One must not be . . . one must not . . ." It seemed to him now that his life had been composed of "must-nots."

A rip of icy pellets, sharp as shot, lashed his face. He stopped, howling his rage up at the heavens like a beast, and snowflakes wet his tongue.

He made himself go forward. Advancing toward an invisible line of rifles.

After an hour, as best he could judge, his feet were numb and he could not be certain he was still on the road. The mountain highlands, all moors and swales, had been stripped of timber for great stretches, and he might have been wandering over the barrens, where abandoned mine shafts and air holes swallowed men and deer. He recalled reading of the servant girl, with child and unmarried, who had thrown herself into a deserted shaft and been found a year later by out-of-work miners poaching coal on company ground. That was just before the war, and everyone thought the girl had run off with her sweetheart.

Mocking himself and his fears, Robert insisted he was still upon the road and that he knew exactly where he was. He drew one leg from a drift, plunged it in front of him, then hauled the other leg up from behind.

With a curse, he hurled the useless bag away.

He had struggled to have faith that, should he die in battle, he would see Charlotte thereafter. Yet, ache though he might, he really could not believe he would ever see her again, not anywhere in eternity, not in the mortal form and flesh he had loved. He did not want to commune with glistening spirits. He wanted to hold the living woman in his arms, his love, to defy death and time and all the iron laws that left him empty.

He stopped again, on a windswept height, and shook his freezing paw at the vacant sky.

"You took her," he cried. "You took her, and you had no right. She never did a thing to you . . . she never . . ."

But his mouth was frozen now, and the words emerged in a childish muddle, and it would have taken God to understand.

He wept and walked. He had not known that a man could be broken and defiant at once. What you saw in prisoners was spite and, sometimes, hatred. Even war had not revealed everything that was in a man.

He did remember that it was Christmas Eve, and the story of the Infant crossed his mind, of other cold journeys and humble lodgings of the sort he had come to know. But he was an educated man who had taken a university degree and read the law for a year before the war called him, and he knew that Palestine was not so cold as this, and that the snow did not fall heavily there, if it fell at all, and that he would have been glad to see his own son born in a stable, if his love had been alive to be the mother.

He began to think he truly might die, and he wondered if that was what he had wanted all the while. Certainly, he had wanted it when last he went into battle, with Charlotte locked inside his frozen heart. He had determined to spend his life, but at the final moment, when the sword came swinging down, his body swerved on its own. The pistol in his right hand thrust up and fired, just as the blade tore through his other sleeve, slicing through flesh and muscle and breaking the bone. The Confederate officer, who had sought to rid him of his life, fell with a startled look, shot through the neck. And then the surgeon had taken off the arm, apologizing briefly for the necessity, since Robert was an officer. And the chloroform was in short supply and reserved for serious wounds. He screamed under the saw, despite himself. And then his soldiering days were behind him, and the hospital would not kill him, either. Now he was here and needlessly alive.

And if he wanted to die, if that was it, why not just stop? His legs marched on, impossibly heavy, as if turned to ice themselves. He bent forward, clutching his hat to his head as the wind grew stronger still. His fingers froze. And he wondered if life had any sense at all.

CATHERINE WAS ASHAMED. She had stayed too long at the Reillys' and had eaten too much of their food. Mother Reilly, clutched by kindness, had asked her in along with the child and no one in the family had counted the slices of bread or skims of butter that crossed her plate, or the biscuits and jam that came after. The Reillys were true Christians, though old Mattie liked a drink. Poor as any they were, though, with the boys both gone to the war and sending back little money, nor was old Mattie any longer a man in his prime. He still had the miner's will and ways in him, but his breath was short and his back had a permanent bent.

She had eaten too much of their holiday bits, all wicked greed, rubbing her fingertip in butter for the infant to gum. Torn between her pride and her belly's complaints. She had been hungry, painfully so, after the long climb up from early mass down in Number Five patch. And Gwennie was always famished. Catherine's milk was spotty now, and she could not see how the two of them would get on.

There were no paying jobs to be had. The household positions down in the valley were filled with girls fresh from Cork or Donegal, willing to work for room and board and little over. Nor would an employer have taken her even on those terms, not with a child. Catherine would have swallowed the last of her pride and cleaned slops for the pennies in it, but of charwomen there was a surfeit, too, and only fallen women went to the laundries.

Not one of the Reillys had said a word, or looked askance, or hinted with one breath that she had eaten more than her allotted share. Oh, perhaps she hadn't taken so much, after all, but she felt as if she had robbed the last crumb from their mouths. Pat would not have allowed it, for he had been proud, too. The only bad moment, really, the only bit of awkwardness, hadn't had a thing to do with the food Mother Reilly had laid out in all her goodness. It had come when old Mattie told Catherine, yet again, that Gwendolyn was an English name and not proper for the child. He said that had her Pat been there, he would have pitched a fit. And tears had come to her eyes, not over the name, which she had chosen from a lovely poem in a book, but at the thought of Pat. He had never "pitched a fit" at her, not ever. Anyway, Gwendolyn wasn't an English name, it was Welsh. But that would have been taken all the worse, so Catherine didn't say a thing. Then Annie Reilly pressed her not to be shy and to sugar her coffee properly, since it was Christmas, after all, wasn't it?

Nor had she wanted to return to the lonely house, as loathe as she was to leave it, as leave it she must and would. In eight days, that would be, for the dunny-man in the black coat from Mr. Thorpe's counting house had given them a grace through the holidays, but she and the child were to be gone without fail the morning after New Year's day. The collector had hinted she might have another week's grace besides, and she understood his offer all too well. She would have liked to slap him, as he deserved, but she had feared losing the days already granted.

She had eaten too much of the Reillys' holiday hoardings, but still she was hungry and still less a woman in body than she had been scant months before, for the pantry box had dwindled and the last of the money was gone. There was talk of a pension, but talk it was and no more. Only scraps of kindness got her and Gwennie through. Thanks be, Mrs. Casey had invited her to share the family's Christmas dinner next day. And go she would, to shame herself again.

No sooner had she tucked the infant into the cradle by the hearth and banked the coals, adding a few more from the scuttle, than she got into Pat's old coat again and threw her shawl around her. Even with the child, the house was lonely. Its four tiny rooms seemed as huge as those of the mansions in the valley. She had lingered too long as a guest only to hide from the enormous hollowness of it, and now she found she was not quite able to bear it, not just yet. Perhaps, she thought, it would have been better had she been one of those women who had a taste for the whisky. For all the good propriety had done her. Propriety and books. As if she thought herself a very queen.

She went back out onto the front porch, careful not to let the door slam hard. Pat had always hated a slamming door. Besides, it would wake the child, and she did not want a child's company now.

Pat, her Pat. How hadn't she troubled him? She wanted him to be genteel, and to scrub the last trace of coal-black from under his nails before he came to her in the dark, and now she saw that she had asked too much, too swiftly, and that he had been a gentle boy and willing. Always willing, Pat had been. And as kind as any man upon the earth.

She ached for all that had been given and taken away.

The snow lashed her. A skilled miner and no mere laborer, Pat had got her the single house let by the company at the high end of the patch. Every other house but one was doubled to another, and the other single house belonged to the Number Seven pit boss. House proud, they called her then, the strange girl married in from the Number Five patch. And the charge had been true enough, though false it was when they said she read so much she neglected her household chores. She would put her house next to any for cleanliness. Even now.

For what little it mattered.

When the news came, their kindness had come out, though. But kindness must have an end upon this earth, and rare was the family that had a bit to spare. Nor would she take charity, but insisted on doing something to earn what they gave, if only their washing. And the black water ruined her hands, the hands of which her Pat had been ever so proud. Why had she deviled him so? Oh, they had gotten on well enough, with never a fight and rarely a squabble, nor did Pat ever raise his hand to her. They had known their private joys, and joys they were. But Catherine was sorry for every word that could not be recalled, for every slight complaint and each hint of disappointment that ever had crossed her face.

She barely felt the cold, although the snow twisted under the eaves of the porch and covered her over. She marked that the storm had already erased her homeward footprints. Brushing the cold wet from her face, she leaned her shoulders against the door.

All the lights in the world had gone out, except for a lamp upstairs in the Fitzgeralds', just over the way. Young Frankie was sick and Molly would be up watching. On any other night, Catherine would have seen the light clearly. Now it was only a faintness in the snow, almost a thing imagined.

She had always imagined too much, dreamed too much, and now the real love given her was gone.

She stepped forward to the edge of the porch and set a bare hand to the railing. Her fingers cut down through inches of snow and found a layer of ice upon the wood. And the railing was loose. That needed to be seen to. Pat would never have tolerated such a thing. He had been an orderly man.

With her hand closed over the ice in self-mortification, she stared into the tempest. Bullets of snow narrowed her eyes and struck her cheek, but the sting only did her good, for she was willing to feel anything other than the loneliness. She began to pray, aloud. Her pitch was not of a level to be heard by her neighbors, not on such a night. But the dark beyond the rush of snow might hear her, and whatever lay beyond the dark.

"Holy Mary," she began, "I know we're not to pray for self-ish matters. But there's nothing left to us now. If not for me, for the child then. For she's innocent. Thy will be done, and that of Your Blessed Son. But help us. I don't know where we'll go, or what we're to do. Help us, and I'll never dream of being more than I am again, or of rising above my station. I'll bear the loneliness, by Your Grace. But don't punish the child for my sins." She shut her eyes tightly, like a little girl making a wish, then said, "Amen."

And then she was cold, and she went in. The child was still asleep by the fire, its cheeks ruddy with the heat, if not with health. Catherine was weary enough, but not yet ready to sleep. For the passage to sleep crossed the vast loneliness of her bed, an emptiness so great not even the child could fill it. Her longings pierced her, and her thoughts strayed toward sin.

There were nights when she awoke and thought she felt her husband beside her. She imagined she could smell him in the dark.

She sat by the fire, chilled through now, although she had exchanged the cold for the warm. Twice she coughed, and coughing always alarmed her. For her mother and sister both had been taken off by the galloping consumption, with her father dead down the shaft not long thereafter, as if the broken-hearted man had willed it. If she were to go, what would become of the child?

She smiled, bitterly, at herself. For she knew she would not be let off so easily. No quick, wan death would come for her. She had her penance to do upon the earth.

She rose and lit the lamp, hoping to read. She had to be shy with the oil, for there was no more in the can, but she could not read by the low light of the coals.

What had she done to deserve penance? She was young, and with the very heart torn from her, and hadn't every one of her sins been small? Was God so hard?

She unpinned her hair and let it fall over her shoulders,

then tried to read a book that had been lent her. But her thoughts were haunted and insistent.

There was no fairness in any of it, no more in Heaven than upon the earth. No justice for any who lacked the purse to buy it. Doubtless the rich had the bigger houses above as they did below, and plenty to eat and no hearts worth the breaking.

She was a proud woman, Catherine Delaney, and as she sat by the fire and Christmas Eve slipped past midnight into Christmas morn, she mocked herself for the shabbiness of her prayers. What was it, after all, but superstition?

She needed a miracle. But the times were modern and sour, and miracles were tales from long ago.

A drowse slipped over her. The infant was tired and contented, and neither mother nor child awoke at the first few knocks on the door. Only the second attempt, a pair of blows no stronger than a child's, began to rouse her.

Suddenly, she leapt from her chair. What was it? Not the Fitzgeralds' little Frankie? Surely not. Not that, not on Christmas Eve.

She rushed to the door and opened it.

A man teetered before her, covered in snow. He might have made her laugh had he not frightened her. His eyes seemed tiny and faint, as if struggling with life itself, and his mouth strained to form the words he wished to say.

At last, he managed the single word, "Please."

Our Simple Gifts

After an instant's dread of what the neighbors might think, Catherine stepped forward to help the stranger inside. She reached to take his arm, but the sleeve was empty.

HE WAS A tall man, too large for her chair, so she tugged him along and helped him into her husband's, just across the fire from her own spot and the cradle. No one had been allowed to sit in that chair since the news came, but there was no helping it now. She told herself that Pat would understand.

The traveler muttered something she could not make out, then his eyes closed and his body slackened. The heat off the hearth melted the snow from his clothing and boots, from his face and beard, and soon he was streaming water onto the floor. Catherine ran for what rags she had and spread them around the chair. Then she remembered what the colliers said about the cold and the way it worked on the flesh when you labored too long above ground in the winter. Gently, she drew the glove from the man's single hand.

The flesh was discolored and stiff. She kneaded it softly, worrying what it would mean to any man who lost consciousness missing one hand and woke to find he was bound to lose the fingers from the other. Then she paused to draw off his boots, worried about all the many bits and pieces of him, and an awkward business it was, for he was dead to the world and could not help her. She nearly pulled him out of the chair, and she slipped once for all the wet and hurt her knee. Next, she rolled off his stockings, which were far too fine for such wanderings, and she swung his feet a bit closer to the fire. Not too close, though, for she recalled that too much heat was a danger, as well. She swallowed her pride and shame alike, rubbing his toes and soles. Ungodly white they were, with pink patches. And two toes blue at the tips. She handled his feet more roughly than she had his hand, hurrying. Then she rose and pulled off his hat, scattering melt.

She saw him truly for the first time then and realized he was young. Despite the strain on his face, as if his dreams were horrid, she did not think him more than twenty-five. If as old as that. Not five years older than she was herself. She thought he might even be handsome, if ever his face unclenched.

Kneeling by his side, she tried again to warm the stiffness from his fingers. It was nearly a terror to her now to think of him, or of any man, without a single hand to help him through his days. Unreasonably, she began to feel that it would be her fault if he were to lose the hand or its fingers.

She rubbed too hard, or perhaps it was his dreams. The traveler groaned. She could have wept to see the young face on him, and the sleeve hanging sodden and empty, and to look at the pale hand in her own. Even punished by the cold, it was clear the hand did not belong to a working man. It had only the sort of callouses a man gets when he plays at labor, not the sort she remembered from her nights. If ever this one had gone down the mines, he had not stayed there long.

But she did not think he had gone down the pits at all, not ever, for his uniform was fine of cloth and made by a master's hand. Wet as the Monday washing, you could still tell that much about it. For a moment she had the cruel thought that such a one as this wouldn't need the hand so badly, for he'd likely have a servant to attend to even his private matters.

She reddened in shame at herself, for she had never thought of herself as cruel. Foolish, yes, and blind at times. Even impatient and mean. But not cruel.

His hand seemed the saddest thing she had ever seen.

"Holy Mary," she prayed again, "if you have no time for me nor mine, then let the poor boy have his hand. He can't deserve such doings, and look what's been taken already."

She saw no change in the fingers, no least return of color. They might have belonged to a corpse. Then she remembered something else, other advice about remedies, and she blushed.

But her blush and her shame did not stop her. Determined, Catherine rose up on her knees and began to unbutton her shirtwaist. Then she drew up the cloth beneath. Watching his closed eyes and dreading their opening, she lifted his hand and spread it across her stomach.

She shuddered, but not only from the cold, and she bent and her own eyes closed. She righted herself by an act of will and closed both hands over his hand, flattening it tightly against her, telling it to take the warmth from her. She had to fight down memories that had no place here and other thoughts that could never belong here or anywhere else. She held his hand against her flesh and prayed. And when her thoughts grew too disordered, she said an invisible rosary, repeating the words again and again, even as her body trembled. Tears had been pouring over her face for several minutes, but she had not realized it until the sharpness of salt stung her lips.

She pressed his hand even more tightly to her flesh, pushing herself against him and breathing deeply, almost gasping. She repeated the sacred chant, perhaps as much to defend herself as to help the young man in the chair.

When one of his fingers moved, she nearly fainted. Then another stirred, and more tears burst from her. She looked at his eyes in alarm, but they remained sealed. After pressing his hand against her a moment longer, she wrenched it away and wrapped it in a dry rag.

A wild feeling of gratitude overwhelmed her and she could not make an end of her weeping. She patted the fingers that had somehow come back from the dead.

Rising to her feet, she set her back to the man and the fire in order to tuck herself in and button her shirtwaist again.

It gave her as great a start as a gun going off when he muttered, "Charlotte."

She closed the last button and turned toward him. His eyes had not opened—could eyes freeze shut? But his lips and the muscles in his cheeks and jaw were testing the return of life and feeling.

Suddenly, his eyes opened. They were of a startling blue.

"How . . . where?" The words were as clumsy as if mouthed by a baby. But Catherine understood.

"You're in the Number Seven patch, sir. That's Mr. Thorpe's Number Seven, mind. And lucky you are to be in it at all, I can tell you."

"How did . . . how did I . . ." He struggled to move his limbs. It was like watching a rusted machine try to start itself.

She had to know one thing. And she banished shyness to learn it. Stepping between the puddles, she took him by the hand and tested the fingers.

"Can you feel this?" she asked. "And this?"

He nodded. Five times.

She had forgotten to wipe away her tears. Remembering of a sudden, she dropped his hand and lifted both of her own palms to her face. She did not know how much he had seen or understood. Or remembered.

She became a woman of propriety again, fiercely so, and fussed about with the rags on the flooded floor.

"Thank you," the young man said, in a strained voice.

She shrugged him off. "It's someone other than me you'd best be thanking. And you're a fool and a disgrace, whatever your name may be, for wandering over the hills on a night like this."

The infant began to shriek, unable to endure these tones of normalcy.

"And one more thing," she said. "My name isn't 'Charlotte.' It's Catherine Delaney, thank you."

THE WOMAN TOOK up the child in the crook of her elbow and disappeared. He heard her climbing stairs he could not see. When she returned, layers of clothing hung over her free arm.

"Here," she said. "You'll be sick to death. Put these on. They're not so fine as you may be used to, and short in the leg they may be, but they're clean as any. They'll do 'til yours come dry."

Cranky-limbed, he reached to take the clothing from her, but at the last moment she hesitated to give them over. Her face clouded. Then she put on a smile that even he could see was willed, not felt, and she dropped the clothing on the chair by the cradle.

"Thank you," he told her again, struggling with the strangeness of his jaw and cheeks. He remembered little after shouting at the sky, and did not know if he had come to this place under his own power or had been found and brought in. "My name's Robert. I'm sorry if—"

"Just call when you're decent," she cut him off. "But not so loud as to tell the whole patch you're here, if you please. For you'll have to leave before the light comes up, or I'll never live it down." And then she marched off round a corner.

He had just gotten used to dressing himself with one arm and had even changed his style of cravat to one he could wrap loosely, but now every one of his limbs was guilty of flagrant disobedience. His head was muddled, too. As if he had drunk that Irishman's whisky, and more. He remembered a wrenching, turbulent dream, in which his love had come to him in flesh and blood, but he could not recall much that was recent and real.

Catherine Delaney. Irish, of course. Bit of a brogue, but not vulgar. He would have to watch his tongue.

For the first time since he awoke, a smile tested his face. If he had to come to his senses after a bad spell of anything, he could have done worse than to awaken with such a woman before him. He had barely seen her, or anything in the room, with clarity. But he had a sense of her that told him she would have stood out in any crowd or congregation. With her long red hair streaming as she left the room. And those no-nonsense eyes—were they green?—that demanded attention and obedience.

He got out of every last bit of his clothing, as if he were back in camp and not in a stranger's home, and drew on the suit of underclothing. It was short in the arms and legs, but hung loosely from his shoulders. The woman's husband was a well-muscled fellow, that much was certain. A miner, naturally.

Robert wondered if the man was away at war or simply off on a tear. Then he began to pull on the trousers and had difficulty with his balance. His legs seemed dead, yet they prickled all over.

He paused to regain his equilibrium, clutching the trousers against his chest. Of a sudden, he noticed how poorly made they were, almost pathetic. But he also knew enough about miners to recognize from the thinnish wool that the trousers were the husband's Sunday best. His other garments would be made of rougher cloth.

Robert got himself dressed, if awkwardly, and managed to step in one of the puddles the snow had made on the floor. It soaked the washworn wool of the stocking.

"Are you decent?" a voice whispered. The woman remained out of sight.

"As much as I'm likely to be," Robert said.

She came in then, with her infant in her arms, and he saw with clearing eyes that she was flawless of feature, with cheekbones that might have done for a young empress. She put him in mind of a picture in a book of his sister's, a portrait in three-quarters profile of a woman, done by an Englishman with an Italian name. It struck him that her husband was a fortunate man in his marriage, whatever else in life he might have lacked.

"I'm sorry to be forward and hurrying you," she said, "but it's cold in the back for the child, for the stove's not up."

Yes, of course. Even now, with the war behind him, Robert assumed that every room in a house would be heated, if not with a glowing stove or marble fireplace, then by a vented pipe. He was ashamed of himself, and not for the first time.

She laid the infant back in its low, wooden cradle.

"Here," she commanded, "let me do that. For you're hopeless and helpless as any man, and I don't know how you all get on in the army." She took his heavy, sodden clothing from him and set each item over the irons or draped them over her own chair, which she edged closer to the fire. "It won't do to scorch those fine boots of yours," she said, pulling them back six inches. "Sit down, would you? You were at death's door not half an hour ago, and now you're prancing about like an April lamb. You'll need more rest than that before you go out again."

He wanted to sit down, longed to. But he couldn't very well sit with a lady in the room. Not until she sat herself, and her chair had been taken by his greatcoat and uniform trousers.

"I'll do that," he said, as she began to spread out his underclothing. It made him blush to see it.

The woman, Catherine, was blushing, too. Unless her face was flushed from the heat of the fire. But she waved him off.

"I've seen worse in my life," she told him.

He found himself staring at her as she worked, and his impropriety embarrassed him the moment he realized it. Whether or not she had seen worse, he had no right to stare at anyone who had been so gracious, so decent, as if she were a common woman in the street. Nor did he stare at "common women," either.

Turning away, forcing himself to turn, he looked over the little parlor. Its form matched thousands of other company-built houses throughout the anthracite fields, all shoddy as an army-issued blanket, and only the smallest personal details distinguished one from another. He saw that, despite the slopping mess he had made, the room was kept clean with the strictness of good staff. It was hardly the rumored hovel in which an Irishwoman was said to live. The truth was that he had never set foot in an Irish household, but knew them only from talk or the occasional sanitary report.

He did not see a single sign of Christmas.

A neat stack of illustrated weeklies sat on a chest, though.

"You enjoy reading, Mrs. Delaney?"

"When there's the time for it. It's my only joy these days."

He looked at her questioningly. Then, fearing rudeness, he cast his eyes back down to the pile of journals. His eyes were not yet at their steadiest, but he recognized the banner of *Harper's Illustrated Weekly*.

"And *Harper's*, too," he said.

"Oh, aren't they fine?" she asked. "Though there's more of the war in them now than a body might wish. I'm fondest of the stories and the poems."

"Well, I'm pleased to meet a fellow subscriber."

She seemed to blush again and looked away. "Oh, I'm not so grand as that. Not half. The Casey girl brings them home for me on her free days. She has leave to take them off when

Mr. Thorpe's done with them, for he says they're hardly proper for the women in his family."

"This Mr. Thorpe again," Robert said.

"Oh, he's the one owns the mountain, and everything above and beneath it, too. Bridget Casey's got a fine position under Mrs. Thorpe. Upstairs, at that."

"Well, I'm glad you're so well accommodated with reading material," Robert said. His back ached, which he realized for the first time. As if the pain had been frozen and waiting to thaw.

The woman sighed. "I'll miss them, I will."

"Supply drying up?"

She looked away, toward the fire, showing a profile as fine as any on earth. "It might as well do. We're off the day after the New Year comes in."

"And where are you going, if I may ask?"

She turned to face him then, with an expression of ferocity and pride.

"You may not, thank you."

Her sharpness startled him. "I'm sorry, I—"

"Oh, sit you down and take your rest, would you? For the night's half gone and more, and you'll hardly have two hours before I'm waking you."

He almost smiled at the thought of that face waking him again, then caught himself. His indecency, in the presence of another man's wife, shocked him.

"And how will you know when to wake me?" he asked.

"Oh, my Gwennie has her hours. She'll not let me sleep 'til dawn, that I can promise."

He peered down at the child. He had been so involved in himself, in his discomforts and travails, that he had paid it scant attention. It looked properly a baby to him, although he was no judge of such matters.

Of men and killing, yes. But not of infants.

He stretched, moving the ghost of an arm along with the whole one left him.

"Are your fingers all right, then?" the woman, Catherine, asked.

He wiggled them and smiled. "Amazing, really. I remember them as a block of ice. No feeling at all when I knocked upon your door."

And there it was, in a flood of released memories. He recalled dragging himself up from the buried road, struggling with the steps, and knocking with a dead fist only because he hadn't the voice to shout and beg. But there the memories stopped again. He could not bring them forward.

But he could go back. He remembered crossing the flat of the heights, afraid all sense of direction had left him, and then he was flirting with Charlotte in the snow, and she kept a few steps ahead of him, always a few steps ahead, teasing, laughing at him, her beauty as pale as the snow, and he followed her and called out, and finally lost her and found himself at a gate left askew and beyond it a pair of shutters bleeding light.

Hadn't he dreamed of her? He closed his eyes and tried to

bring her back. But something—something very deep within—had changed in him. He saw, with metal certainty, that he had lived too long in a hollow dream, playing a game of pretend that was only a mockery. He had imagined he would find Charlotte living still, if only he loved hard enough and looked. But now—it was the strangest thing—he knew that she was gone, and gone forever. He had left her on those heights. Or had she left him? And his dream had run elsewhere.

He opened his eyes to the light of the dying fire. A crackle of flame reflected off the tin of a picture frame.

Pat Delaney.

Dear God.

Pat Delaney, photographed in a new, ill-fitting private's uniform, with the mark of a Pottsville studio at the bottom. An overgrown child, trying to look stern and soldierly.

Pat Delaney, whose face was shot away and his brains spilled out, halfway across the field where Robert had thought to lose his life and merely lost an arm.

He turned so sharply he nearly tumbled over. He had to clutch the back of a chair to steady himself.

"Your husband, Mrs. Delaney?" he asked, although he knew the answer as surely as he had ever known anything.

Pat Delaney, who had been a good and quiet soldier, dependable and not a drunkard, ever writing letters home until the boys teased him raw. Robert understood that writing now. And he knew that Patrick G. Delaney, three-year enlistment, assigned to Company D, Robert's own, had never seen his infant in its cradle.

"Yes," she said. "My husband. He was killed in September."

If Robert's body was stiff and slow, his mind was working admirably. He understood the woman's turn of anger now, when asked where she was moving. She was being evicted. And she had nowhere to go, nor a penny to take her, like as not.

It seemed impossible to him. Such matters had always been far away, business affairs concerning other men or brief reports in a newspaper, doubtless exaggerated.

How could such a thing be allowed?

He turned on her, as if ready to grasp her and shake her. As if she were at fault and not the world.

"Mrs. Delaney," he said. "Do you have a place to go when you leave here? You must answer me."

"It's none of your—"

"Answer me, madame!" The sound of his own voice shocked him.

She crumpled at his tone and could not face him. "We'll move in down the way with the Reillys for a bit. A week or two, then I don't know."

She sat down in the chair she had invited him to occupy, burying her face in her hands. He expected to hear sobs, but in another moment, she put herself right. As if the palms of her hands had applied a fresh varnish of spunk.

Standing up, she said, "You'll want to sleep a bit. I haven't a

spare blanket, I'm sorry, but you'll be warm enough by the fire."
She felt his uniform tunic to gauge its dampness, then turned
it inside out, after which she did the same with his greatcoat.

"This Mr. Thorpe . . . I take it he's a hard man? Disliked by
the miners and their families?"

"Oh, he's far and away not the worst, as I hear tell. The pit boys
say he's better than the run of the owners north of the mountain.
And he gave us grace to stay on through the Christmastide."

"I think this is infamous. You . . . a fallen soldier's wife . . ."
She reared up at that. "I'll not be pitied," she told him.

"But you pitied me . . . when I appeared at your door."

"That was different," she snapped. "And Christmas Eve it
was. Now, be a gentleman, won't you please, and go to sleep."

She put out the lamp, then went out with her child and a
candle. He heard her footsteps on the invisible stairs again,
and her tread was slow and weary, as if all the fight had gone
out of her the moment she left the room. Stiff as one of the
ancients, Robert poked up the coals in the fire. Satisfied by
the bloom of heat, he sat down and went to sleep instantly.

HE JUMPED WHEN she touched him. As if a sentry had
sounded an alarm.

"Wake up," she said. "For you'll have to be off, I'm sorry."

"Yes . . . of course," he said, rousing himself. She had stirred
his shoulder from behind, so he did not wake to the sight of

her face this time. But he got the smell of thin coffee in his nostrils, and the fire had been fed until it warmed and lit the room. He had slept as the woman worked.

If he had dreamed, he could not remember it. His sleep had been deep and hard, yet its brevity did not leave him addled very long. In a moment, he was yawning, stretching out his good arm and the ghost.

"You were sleeping like a great bear," she said. "I let you be as long as I could. But you have to go, or there'll be talk. For by rights I shouldn't even have let you in."

"It was an act of mercy. Of great charity."

"Tell that to old Mother Connelly down the way, and see where it gets you. Or to Father Daniel himself."

"It was an act of kindness. On Christmas Eve." She swept into view and he saw the slender loveliness of her in full. "Merry Christmas, Mrs. Delaney."

"And a Merry Christmas to you, Mr. Robert. Or is it General Robert or such like?"

"Plain 'Robert' will do."

She laughed like a girl, but spoke in a woman's voice. "Robert may do, but hardly plain. Here. I made you a toast on the fire, and coffee's in the kettle. I'll go out for a bit now, so you can put on your soldier suit again. Give a whisper when you're ready. And mind the baby in the cradle there."

She took a candle against the last, thick dark beyond the

doorway, then paused on the threshold. "Keep the woolen stockings, would you? For your own aren't fit for winter on the roads."

"Thank you," he said. "I will."

The toast had been dipped in fat, the coffee reboiled. But it was lovely to him. A lovely Christmas breakfast. He had not felt himself so alive in months.

He gobbled the toast and swilled down the scalding liquid like an old sergeant of regulars. Then he dressed, pulling on the lovely warmth of his uniform trousers, their wool the slightest bit scorched from the hearth and smoke-scented. The greatcoat was still damp and heavy, and the boots had stiffened. He left the coat on the chair a moment longer.

"Mrs. Delaney," he called, softly.

In a moment, she was back by the fire. With a shiver. Then she looked at him and smiled. "But aren't you the dandy one? And to think how you looked the night back! Now you're fit to charm all the belles at your Christmas ball."

He smiled. "I shall value that as a great compliment, madame." And he bowed.

But when his eyes came back up, he saw a look near sorrow on her face.

After all, what did she have to smile about? On Christmas morning or any other morning?

"Mrs. Delaney, I won't offer you money—"

"I *want* no money, I wouldn't—"

"—because I know you wouldn't take it. But thank you. With all my heart."

And he meant it. For his heart seemed oddly alive again, and lighter than it had been in many months. Or longer.

"Your thanks I will accept, and wish you well, Mr. Robert."

"Just plain 'Robert.' Please."

She laughed again. For just that moment, she sounded as though she hadn't a care in the world. "Robert, then. But not plain. For that you'll never be. Now out with you. The light will come up and I'll never get past the shame." She picked up his greatcoat with both hands and held it out to him.

He put it on, buttoning it adeptly with one hand. She watched his fingers with a concentration that struck him as uniquely feminine.

"Well, I'll slip off, then."

She shook her head. Slightly. "Would you . . . oh, it will sound like the strangest thing . . ."

"What is it?"

"Would you shake my hand, Robert?"

He smiled. "Of course. Good Lord, if that's all . . ."

She took his hand in both of hers, but she did not shake it, not properly. Instead, her fingers played over every inch of it, slowly, almost as if sneaking. As if she were measuring it to make a counterfeit or, perhaps, a glove. Trying to remember every joint and fold of flesh.

Abruptly, she let him go. And he realized the high corners of the room were not as dark as they had been.

"Out with you, now," she said, stepping to open the door. "And fare thee well."

She peered outside, eyes scouting along the pale and perfect street, then motioned for him to pass her.

He stopped at the sight of the gray, glistening world, at the shock of the huge, dry cold. The storm had passed, leaving a buried earth behind.

"My footsteps," he whispered, coming close to her face and catching the almond scent of her for the first time. Rich in his cold-stung nostrils. "They'll see my footsteps."

"Go to the middle of the road there. Where it's blown thin already. It'll take off your traces soon enough. And I'll clean along the go-through."

He looked at her one last time and found wet, porcelain eyes. Then she looked away, and turned her back, and shut the door behind her.

HE WORKED HIS way down through the mining patch and no dog barked until he reached its end. Then he followed the open lane, white between the still-black trees, with the evergreens warmed with snow and the naked birches shivering in the meaner ground, and the earth was pale and the sky still dark overhead. When he left the grove, he took the downward fork, away from the black outline of the colliery, and he saw the last stars before him, one far brighter than any of the others. It struck him, as he strode toward its light, that he was not the first man to follow a star on Christmas morn, but then he dismissed such a comparison as vain and unforgivable.

Slowly at first, then with wonderful speed, the earth and sky brightened around him. Even the rising piles of coal waste and the breaker towers and tipples had been whitewashed with a gracious, even hand. He knew exactly where he was now, knew the way with certainty. The going was a slog, but hardly a threat to life and limb. The terrors of the night seemed almost laughable now, and he wondered how much danger he really had faced.

Then he recalled enough to make him shudder.

But he was going forward now, not back. It was a long way, miles, down to the main road, past Number Six patch and its colliery, then through Number Five, which was already coming to life in its fairy ring of birches, its chimneys spicing the air with kitchen smoke. Children called out gleefully, while bundled men and women hastened down their gardens to the outhouses, each woman with a nightpot in her hand. He smiled at the sheer, glorious life of it, and two intrepid boys on a homemade sled went howling past him.

He felt the bite of the cold, but knew he could bear it. His strength seemed so much renewed that he wondered at the weakness he had cast off. As if it had been a sickness.

Down below, in the town, the first church bells greeted the day. More bells joined in, and soon the long valley echoed with ringing from every church and chapel, from the Episcopal stone belfry he knew so well, from Presbyterian brick and Methodist clapboard, and from the Catholic churches thrown up from scrap lumber in the patches or built from a mountain of tiny contributions to match the other churches in the town.

The rising sun gilded the snow. Even halfway down the mountainside, the view was as spectacular as it was clear. When first he marked the chimney plumes and glimpsed the familiar gables and spires through a gap in the trees, his heart leapt. And then, just at the junction with the main road, he heard sleigh bells.

He recognized the curves of the vehicle from a distance, and the team, and then the driver's posture. It was a wonderful stroke of luck and Robert began to wave.

As the sleigh approached, the driver tugged back on the reins. The runners skittered to a stop and Robert saw a quizzical expression on the young man's face. Behind him, two young ladies in matching fur caps huddled under a pile of traveling blankets.

"Billy, I thought you might offer a fellow a ride. On Christmas morning."

A look of wonder contorted the young man's face and it took him several seconds to form his words.

"Robert!" he cried at last, rising to his feet with the reins in his hands. Then he sat back down in blunt astonishment. "For crying out loud, Robert Thorpe!"

At that, the girls beneath the blankets gasped and leaned sidewards to get a better look at him. He had recognized them as easily as he did the sleigh, Jenny and Clare Carruthers, driving over early from Tamaqua with their brother to spend the day with the Menzies, who had one daughter and two sons of matching age and eligibility.

But they had not recognized him.

Jenny, the elder, had been a rival of Charlotte's. They had flirted at holiday balls and parties before he declared himself. Now she stared at him in bewilderment, eyes settling on the empty sleeve of his greatcoat.

"For crying out loud, get in," Billy said. "Jen, Clarie, make room under those blankets for Robert. I think we can trust the discretion of one of our noble officers returning from the wars."

The girls regarded him with morbid awe, but Robert refused to be daunted. He wished them "Merry Christmas" in a voice as grand as the valley below them and laughed to rival the sleigh bells. Then the morning grew festive, with declarations of wonder and friendships renewed. The girls had a thousand questions, and they asked them all without waiting for the answer to the first one. Billy leaned back and said they'd all stop by the house later and drink some of his father's punch, if Robert had no objections, which he didn't. Then, a mile short of town, Billy told the girls to mind their own business, for crying out loud, and to stop pestering Robert, and he handed back his flask of cherry brandy.

THE TOWN HAD a round-bellied feel, with its Christmas breakfasts behind it and the streets pert with the smell of turkey and goose in a hundred ovens. There were no formal choirs of welcome, but a pack of rambunctious, well-dressed boys went caroling through the streets for unneeded pennies. It was a morning when those abroad in the streets did not merely tip their hats, but smiled and passed a holiday greeting. All glistened.

Robert asked his old acquaintance to let him down a block short of his home. Now, at the last moment, he found he needed time. He had imagined everything a certain way. He must walk up the carriageway and climb the steps old Drummond would have swept clean this one morning, since the maids not let off for the day had been helping Mrs. O'Brien with the dinner preparations since dawn or even earlier. And he would tidy himself one last time in front of the frosted panes, then reach for the bell-pull.

Now, with good-byes bid to the tune of promised visits and Billy's sleigh jangling off, Robert felt a wave of fear, a dread of confidence misplaced amid crumbling worlds.

"Why, Robert!" Mrs. Devereux cried, surprising him with

her voice that never aged, although the hair beneath her bonnet would be white to a paucity. "Your mother never told me you were coming home!"

"Merry Christmas, Mrs. Devereux." He laid his finger over his lips in a salute to secrecy. "I didn't tell her. Or anyone."

Olive Devereux had lived a very long time, and seen much, and she did not even blink at Robert's sleeve. She only said, "What a wonderful surprise! Your mother couldn't have a better present. But I'm delaying you . . . Merry Christmas, Robert. And welcome home."

She smiled, but there were unexpected tears in her eyes.

He began to march, then. His step was not fearful now, as it had been upon too many battlefields, but firm, as if guided by a beacon. He straightened his greatcoat, then re-set his hat.

He passed the corner and saw his house—his home—upon its hillock. His father had built it when Robert was fifteen, and its luxury had been the talk of the county, until more recent contestants had surpassed it. Its gabled towers were decked with snow, the tall central tower where he had played at Ivanhoe and Lancelot, surveying his kingdom, and the twin towers set back on the flanks. The front door was trimmed in greens, with scarlet ribbons.

And then the last minute had fled, and the last step had been taken. He stamped the snow from his boots and pulled the bell cord. Then he rapped with the knocker, for certainty.

Drummond opened the door and recognized him at once.

Robert almost thought he saw a smile cross the old English-man's lips, though that would have been straining the bounds of credulity.

"Master Robert," Drummond said calmly. "Welcome home, sir."

But Amelia had come up behind to see who had come to visit, perhaps expecting her latest beau, and she shrieked to rouse the dead. She threw herself past Drummond and onto Robert's chest, almost suffocating him as she clung to him, and he toted her in through the door.

"Oh, Robbie, Robbie, Robbie . . ." she said, crying and laughing. And he heard his father's voice bark down the hallway.

"Amelia, what the blue blazes—"

Then the father saw the son, and stopped. His father looked older, markedly so, with hardly a trace of black left in his whiskers. His confident expression faltered, and Robert could not tell if it was pain or happiness filling the old man's eyes. Then his father mastered himself and called firmly, "Rose, would you come downstairs, please?"

But mothers know, and Robert's mother was already standing at the head of the stairs, with a hand over her heart.

THEY ALL MADE a terrible fuss, with the maids squirreling about and Mrs. O'Brien coming up from the kitchen for a peek at him, and everyone pretending they didn't notice his missing arm, not a bit, until it made Robert want to laugh out loud. He had never been hugged so abundantly and mercilessly in his life, and even his father permitted himself one crisp embrace.

His mother alternated between radiant joy and weeping. "Oh, Robbie," she said, "I've never had such a gift on any Christmas."

But as soon as he could fairly evade his mother's and sister's caresses, he asked his father if he might see him in his study for a moment.

"Don't you want to dress before our guests arrive?" his father asked.

"Of course, Father. This won't take a moment."

His father smiled, although his eyes still wore a terrible concentration, as if his regained son might prove but a specter. "Well, this must be terribly important. Come along, Robert."

In the study, where the light was always amber, his father took his seat behind his desk with the old, familiar sequence of motions. It was wonderful to see him sitting there, as if nothing had changed in the world.

Robert pushed the door almost shut, to gain a bit of privacy, then stood before the huge desk like a supplicant employee.

"Father, I want you to do something for me. For Christmas. I want you to give me a Christmas gift."

The man with the gray whiskers looked bemused. "Well, the army's made you rather bold, I must say. I can't recall you ever asking for anything outright. Not since you were a child." His father smiled with a corner of his mouth. "Even then, you were too proud to come right out with it." The aging man settled back and the morning light slipped through the shutters, painting his face with diagonal streaks of gold. "I suppose I'd best take this seriously."

"Please, Father. I want you to take it very seriously."

His father forgot himself, just for a moment, and his eyes traveled to the empty sleeve.

"But I don't want you to do it because you feel sorry for me," Robert forged on. "There isn't the least reason for that. I want you to do it because it's the right thing to do."

"I'm sorry if I was tactless, Robert."

"I don't want you to be sorry, Father. I want you to be generous."

The loose skin tightened around his father's eyes. "I don't know whether this business of yours is becoming interesting, or worrisome. I've always considered myself a generous man. Haven't I been?"

Robert plunged ahead. The way he had broken from a walk into a run, lifting his sword to point the way as he led his company toward the enemy breastworks. "Father, there's a widow, a Mrs. Delaney, up in Number Seven patch. Her husband was a soldier in my company, a good soldier. He was killed in the same battle where I—anyway, she's been given notice of eviction. A veteran's widow, Father!" Robert took a deep breath, and launched himself over the barricade. "I want you to let her stay on. And to forego her rent for as long as she wishes to stay there."

A look of genuine astonishment swept his father's face. "Good Lord, boy. A man of my position can't interfere with petty business. It's . . . it's not the way things are done. We have a system, you know. Oh, I'm sorry for the poor woman, of course . . . but, one day, when the company's passed to your hands, you'll under—"

Robert cut his father off, a thing he had never done. "Father, I'm not a 'boy.' And I think I do understand. More than you realize. I don't believe I've ever asked you for a single thing before, not as a man. But now I'm begging you—"

"My son doesn't beg," his father said.

The one thing Robert did not want to do was to tell his father that the woman likely had saved his life. There were other things, too, that would not bear telling. Not now. He wanted this to be a pure, just gift. But in a sudden flush of desperation, he was about to relate his experience of the night before, to try to move this immovable man whom he loved but could not fathom, when the door creaked behind him.

His mother had come into the room. He did not have to look. He knew her presence in that unmistakable way that words will not explain. And then he heard her voice, cheerful, chiding, confident and imperious, all at once.

"Andrew, I am astonished at you. You will do as Robert asks, and you will do it with a good heart. Or I will put on my cape and hat and leave this house until you do."

"Rose, don't be—"

"Don't take that tone with me, Mr. Andrew Thorpe. Or I'll be out that door before you can make one more of your childish faces." Her voice was as buoyant as it was formidable.

"*Please*, Father."

His mother rested a hand upon his shoulder. "Be quiet now, Robert. Your father's making a decision."

He would have stood there, gladly, all the day long, if only his mother's hand stayed where she had placed it.

Abruptly, his father reared up in his chair. With a huge grump that barely masked a groan. He glanced at his wife with a scolded boy's sideward look, then lowered his eyes to his desk in lovely embarrassment.

"This must *not* become a habit, Robert," he said. "The poor must learn discipline and Christian diligence. Why, when your grandfather came to this country—"

His mother laughed, and Robert felt as though she had welcomed him to a new stage of adulthood, letting him sneak a look behind the curtain of his parents' married life. She dropped her hand away, only to lay her arm, lightly, around his waist.

"We're all terribly proud of you, Robert," she said. "And now I think you should bathe."

HE HAD BEEN planning as he walked that morning. He had mapped out and rejected one course of action after another until he saw precisely how the thing must be done, for propriety's sake.

Before he went upstairs to climb into the great enameled tub in his father's dressing room, he slipped along the garlanded hall and down to the kitchen in the cellar.

He gave Mrs. O'Brien and the girls a fright. They had granted themselves a pause in their labors, and Robert's eye, conditioned to register the flash of a distant bayonet, saw the glasses disappear under starched aprons or maneuver behind mixing bowls.

"Mrs. O'Brien!" Robert said. "I can't believe you've grown so wicked! Not offering to share a glass of Christmas cheer with me!"

"We was but putting the sherry to the test," the red-faced woman said, wiping her drenched forehead with her wrist. The kitchen was mercilessly hot. "Before getting up the trifle and the puddings."

"Well, may I test it with you, then? The truth is, I'm still chilled to the bone."

It wasn't sherry at all, but his father's best Madeira. That only made Robert smile. And it did taste damnably good. But he had come with another purpose.

"Miss Casey?" he addressed one of the maids, a wedge-faced girl with colorless hair.

"By your leave, sir."

"Miss Casey, I thought you might assist me with a small problem."

"Sir?"

"Do you happen to know the name of the priest responsible for Number Seven patch?"

"Is it the true-church priest you're meaning, sir?"

"Yes. The Catholic fellow."

"Well, that would be Father Daniel, acourse. For we all must come down to Number Five to hear the mass said."

"Father Daniel? In Number Five patch?"

"By your leave, sir."

He downed the last of the Madeira in his glass. "Miss Casey, you're an absolute angel," he said. "And Mrs. O'Brien? A vintage Madeira really should be drunk up once it's opened. I'd hate to think of it spoiling."

"Sure, and ye've grown to a darling man, Master Robert," the cook told him. "And here we was fearing ye'd come back all sulking and sorrowing."

But Robert was already bounding back up the stairs, leaving a priceless tittering in his wake.

Drummond had prepared his bath with buckets of hot water brought up on the dumbwaiter. The tub steamed and beckoned. And Robert stripped himself down with the anticipation of a mighty pleasure, as if readying himself for a summer swim with the other boys from the row of high houses, though no other house had been so high as Robert's own. He was ever the first to dive from the bank, too. He had always been first, in all things, if only because he assumed it his right to be so.

The old servant had put out fresh linens and Robert's finest dress suit. Robert could smell the naphtha flakes above the few drops of cologne water his father allowed for male baths. The stained-glass window shone wet with steam, and the Turkey towels hung ready. It was all so wonderfully familiar and delicious that Robert wondered how he could have failed to be happy one single day in his life before the war.

And then, to improve upon Heaven, Amelia began to play the piano downstairs. For him. It was his favorite sonata, by Field. Next, her fingers leapt into a holiday reel.

"Have you any other needs at the moment, Master Robert?" Drummond looked dutifully past him, as if Robert were royalty, and had not the least regard for the stump of his arm.

"Yes, I do. Dear, old Drummond. Would you find Murphy, wherever he's gotten to this blessed day, and tell him to harness a horse to the cutter?"

"Will you be going out, sir?"

"No. But I have an errand for Murphy. Tell him he'll have a full week's extra wages in recompense for being disturbed on Christmas Day."

"I fear, Master Robert, that Mr. Murphy may already have begun his celebrations. His condition may be indecorous."

"As long as he can drive to Number Five patch and back, and drop off a letter, he'll do. Would you find him? Please, Drummond?"

"Of course, sir."

Robert would have liked to loll in the lovely warmth of the bath for an hour, calling up more hot water as the tub cooled. But he had already heard the front bell ring once. That would be the rector, who never risked missing the least of the Christmas titbits. And the other guests would tumble in soon enough, and Robert knew and accepted that he would be possessed by one of them after another, and he would endure all that with the best of hearts, only he had a task that wanted completion first.

There was nothing he could decently do, of course, to treat the woman to a feast this day, or even to warm her rooms. Or, he thought, her heart. He would not dare to send her so much as a blanket directly, for any slight gift from him would demand explanation, and he knew enough of his valley to comprehend the ease with which a woman's reputation might be ruined.

At the image of Catherine Delaney's Christmas, the soap, or perhaps the cologne in the water, troubled his eyes. But he finished washing himself, getting as clean as the time allowed, then he learned, again, how difficult it was to pour a bucket of rinse water over himself with a single hand.

The studs for his shirt gave him difficulty and he dropped a back-piece then spent precious minutes searching the floor for it. His vest and frock coat were snug in the chest and shoulders now, and his trousers were loose at the waist, but he managed to put himself together well enough to avoid public shame, though he had to flip his cravat over like a Frenchman's. He gave himself a last inspection in his father's tiltmirror, splashed a few drops of cologne water on his beard, then took the stairs at a gallop.

Drummond stood by the door to bid in the guests. Robert hurried across the parquet, ready to speak, but Drummond simply said, "Mr. Murphy's below, sir, awaiting your instructions. I fear he has been somewhat indulgent."

"Thanks a barrel, Drums," Robert said, exactly as he had said it years before, whenever the servant helped him evade discovery for his lesser infractions.

He almost got away. But Dr. and Mrs. Gottschalk were at the door, and he had to be polite, of course, and that delayed his trip to his father's study five minutes more.

Alone at last and seated at his father's desk, he began to write. At first, he was in too much of a hurry, and he slopped the ink and had to begin again on a clean sheet. But his thoughts were clear, for all his excitement, and the words flowed easily.

He wrote to the priest, over his father's signature, summoning back the language of the law office where he had read for the bar the year before the war. He stipulated that, in recognition of her late husband's services to his country and its flag, Mrs. Catherine Delaney, widow, resident at the Number Seven Colliery settlement (which property, as well as all permanent structures and improvements thereon, was recognized in deed by the Commonwealth of Pennsylvania as claim and parcel of the Thorpe Coal & Iron Company, said deed filed in the County of Schuylkill) was now and hereafter relieved of the obligation to pay any and all rents, costs or fees on her current dwelling and abode; further, said dwelling and abode was to be regarded as the sole and solemn property of Mrs. Catherine Delancy until such time as she might elect to remove herself of her own free will. He added another detail, blotted the sheet, and went into the drawing room to seek his father.

His father was surrounded by guests, of course. Worse, when Robert entered, all those gathered broke into applause, and Judge Putnam called out, "Hail the conquering hero!" Delsy McCord, Amelia's silly and lifelong friend, who had grown up a beauty as empty-headed as ever, affected a swoon. Her collapse into Johnny Drayton's delighted arms created a great stir over by the German tree, where a maid—Miss Casey it was—had been posted between two buckets of water to keep watch over the candles on the branches. The rector immediately flanked Robert with questions about strategy, and old Colonel Masters, who had served in the war with Mexico, leaned on his cane and inquired, loudly, about the belles of Virginia, then proceeded to reminisce about the tawny señoritas of Monterrey. Ambushed and surrounded, Robert wielded his finest manners like a saber until he had cut his way through to his father.

"Father, if I may have just one more moment?" he whispered.

His father held up a glass of punch, the making of which was his jealously guarded prerogative, and asked, entwining cheer and exasperation, "Surely, Robert, other matters can wait now. Our guests . . ."

"One moment, father. Please."

"But can't this wait?"

"No, it has to be done today. For Christmas."

His father shook his head and tutted. "I swear you take after your mother's side, not the Thorpes."

And for one flashing, melancholy moment, as father and son evaded the enthusiasms of family and friends, Robert foresaw the day when his father would no longer mix the punch or complain of a son's baffling whims.

Then they were in the study again, with the door closed firmly this time and his father behind his desk in shifted light, spectacles pinched down on his thickening nose.

His father nodded twice, then looked up sharply.

"You said nothing about a pension."

"I intend to pay it out of my own wages."

"But is that wise? And five dollars a week? To what end, Robert?"

"To a good end, Father."

"The poor must not be coddled. We must set high standards for them, as we do for ourselves."

Robert thought of the fierce mother in the drafty chill of her rooms, and of the determined cleanliness and the carefully ordered weeklies, of the tin-framed photograph, doubtless the only one she possessed of her own beloved, and of the lack of a single spare blanket.

"We don't understand the poor, Father. Neither of us."

"The poor don't need understanding. They need honest work and a sense of responsibility."

"Please, Father. Sign it. It's Christmas." He almost added, "You promised," as a child might.

And his father signed, mumbling about the irregularity of communicating directly with a Catholic priest on this or any other matter.

"It's the best way, Father. The only one, really."

His father blotted the signature, then passed him the letter. "This *must* not become a habit," he warned. "You need to learn to handle the subordinate classes, Robert."

And Robert thought of the men who had followed him, the living and the dead, whose miseries and triumphs he had shared, and he saw his father in a different light again, one that had little to do with the silver-gold sifting through the shutters, and he felt a pang of sorrow in his heart that cut as deeply as a loved one's death. For he saw that he had passed his father by, and his father's age, which a great war had shattered. That, too, was a form death took.

"No, Father. It won't become a habit. Will you excuse me?"

"Robert, I must insist that you join our guests. They're all anxious to see you, you know."

"I won't be five minutes. I promise." And he turned to push along his grand design.

But as he opened the door, his father called to him.

Robert turned. His father held his spectacles before him, as if frozen in mid-gesture, and his eyes were no longer those of a colliery lord.

"I'm very fond of you, you know," he told his son. "And proud."

"Thank you, Father."

"Now go and finish your nonsense. Our guests are waiting."

MURPHY HAD ENTHRONED himself down in the kitchen, where he clearly had hoped to find succor and something to drink. But Drummond had given Mrs. O'Brien the strictest orders that the coachman's sobriety, such as it was, must be preserved. As Robert came down the back stairs, he heard the fellow complaining about the endless, boundless, matchless and vicious sufferings he had to endure for his weekly pittance.

"I'm sorry you're so unhappy in my father's employ, Mr. Murphy," Robert said from the doorway.

The Irishman twisted and rose, and nearly bolted out of the high little window. "Oh, Master Robert, it weren't but a figger o' speaking. A test o' Mrs. O'Brien's own loyalties, it was."

"Get on with you," the cook said.

"Of course, Mr. Murphy," Robert said. "I'd complain myself, if someone interrupted my Christmas revels. But look here. I need you to take a letter to Number Five patch for me. You are to put it directly—directly, you understand—into the hands of Father Daniel. If he has gone elsewhere for the day, go after him and find him." Robert dug into the purse that still contained his back pay and took out a twenty-dollar gold piece. "Give this to Father Daniel, with my father's compliments, for the good of his flock on Christmas day. And tell him that my father respectfully requests that the news in the letter be communicated to the concerned party today."

"Oh, that's a great lot for the remembering," Murphy said. "And didn't Old Drums not say something or t'other as to a week's full and stipendious wages, what I was to have for the confiscations o' my holiday freedom?"

Robert reached into his purse again. "Under the circumstances, Mr. Murphy, I think that offer wanted in generosity." He put a second gold piece into the man's palm. "Come back and put the horses up before you resume your celebration."

Murphy gathered himself and thrust out his barrel chest. "And when did I ever fail in me care o' the horses, Master Robert? Why, I recall when you was no bigger than—"

Robert hastened back upstairs, pausing only to inspect himself in the hallway glass, whereupon he straightened his cravat. He launched himself—not dutifully, but joyously—into the crowded drawing room.

He was asked about the war and his plans, queried about suspected amorous adventures among the enemy or in rare and distant cities, and wasn't that the worst Christmas storm last night? But followed by a lovely Christmas Day, mind you. Between the minor chords of a whisper of sympathy for the loss of his betrothed the summer before, he overheard Mrs. Dalrymple complain of the emotional strain she had endured in letting her Irish maid go just before Christmas. The girl had been stealing leftover food and taking it home, and weren't the Irish hopeless? The rector explained to Robert that, based upon his detailed study of the career of the great Napoleon, the generals on both sides of the present war had not the least inkling of the proper methods of campaigning. If he, the rector, were in command . . . Judge Putnam clapped Robert on the back and clinked glasses so hard he spilled punch on the Brussels carpet. And Delsy McCord stared at him with great cow eyes, sighing so loudly he could hear her across the room.

Then Drummond slid back the panel doors and stepped aside, rigorous as the young grenadier he once had been, clearing the way for Robert's father to offer his mother an arm—with the precise gesture he employed year after year— and lead the party into the double dining room, where the two great tables bore silver enough for a treasurehouse.

To his red-faced chagrin, Robert found that his mother— or perhaps Amelia—had placed him next to Delsy McCord, who must have known in advance, for her gown had slipped noticeably lower on her shoulders. But after he had guided her chair just the right distance toward the brocade of the tablecloth—which he thought he did quite artfully, given his minor limitation—and endured the "accidental" brush of Delsy's hand, he decided, "Oh, what the devil . . ." Delsy had to have her Christmas, too. He resolved to charm the daylights out of her and to keep her champagne glass full.

But first came the lull between the seating and the serving, as punch cups thoughtlessly brought to table were drained and handed off and each guest grew accustomed to his or her neighbors, measuring whether their given seats reflected a rise or fall in status across the year, although Robert knew his mother didn't give the matter a passing thought.

And in that moment of settling and small confusions, Robert's heart slipped away. The handsome scents of food and the gleaming opulence drove his thoughts to cold encampments and sick wards, to sentries tramping back and forth in the snow, chins tucked down behind their scarves and collars. And he thought of Charlotte, whose grave he would visit when the guests had gone away. She was a beautiful memory now, but a memory and no more. Then he thought of the widow, Catherine, and knew that he would see her again, and that it would be by the light of day, and that no shame would ever touch her, not ever again.

"*Robert!*"

At the sound of his mother's voice, he snapped back to the present.

"Robert," she repeated, but more softly. "Your father was speaking to you."

"Sorry," he said hurriedly. He looked up along the great table, over the silver domes and past the Dresden centerpiece, between the gilt candlesticks set out on the cloth and the crystal chandelier. He looked up to where his father sat, and met a look of concern so slight a stranger would not mark it, yet one so great it tore at Robert's heart. "I'm sorry, Father."

"I only wished to ask, Robert, if you would honor us with the first Christmas toast."

Embarrassed by his inattention to his father, Robert attempted to rise too swiftly. Drummond rushed to grasp his chair. He felt the seat pull away from the back of his knees and steadied himself. And he picked up his glass of champagne.

The glass stopped him for a moment. Cut of Bohemian crystal, the stem was clear but the bowl was tinged pale rose and etched with vines of immaculate delicacy. It astonished him that anything so fine could still exist in the world through which he had passed. He suffered the muted echo of cannon and shouting men, heard mortal cries, and wavered. Then Charlotte's voice bid him follow her homeward through the snow one last time, on a journey of forgiveness and farewell.

And another voice, thrilling in its appetite for life, said, "Robert, then. But not plain."

He was not certain he could depend upon his powers of speech, or even on the valor of his eyes, but he lifted the glass high and looked at all the kind, expectant faces.

"May we . . ." he began, ". . . may we only learn to love one another. And merry Christmas!"

Tannenbaum

TARTLED BY THE sound of the shot, the men of the company looked up from their chores. Those lucky enough to be gathered by a tent stove lowered tin mugs of coffee or hands of cards, waiting for a second shot to confirm the need to rise and grasp their rifles. But the harsh wind from the sea carried the sound away, leaving nothing in the ear but the wind's own keening. Sand blew into kettles from which it had just been scrubbed and the low pines surrounding the camp waved their branches.

"Oh, my God," a voice cried. "Oh, my dear God."

And the soldiers ran toward that voice, as if rallying to a flag, and the voice cried out again, in sorrow and wonder. The men gathered with murmurs and sudden gasps, but soon fell silent. Old comrades stood shoulder to shoulder, gaping. The wind skimming the dunes and slapping their tents felt unnaturally bitter, and those who had not thought to take up their jackets as they rushed out into the afternoon stood goose-fleshed beneath red woolens.

"It's Billy Barrett," a bearded private said, speaking for all, in a voice that pierced the wind.

Gustave Tannenbaum—"Dutch" or "Gus" to his comrades—did not push toward the front of the crowd. He had seen enough. Gus had known what had happened the instant he heard the shot. He could not have explained to another of the men how he had known, but at the sound of the discharge his heart had crumpled inward. He had lived long enough to know that many things in life refuse to be explained, and despite the education for which his late and beloved father had paid, he had learned to accept that not every question had an answer.

Gus had known that Billy Barrett had taken his own life the instant it happened, although he had felt no inkling of the deed a moment before. Now he told himself that he should have known, that he should have done something to prevent it. But he had not known, and he had done nothing, and now the sad boy lay dead. Billy, who had never made fun of him, who had been the butt of jokes himself, and who had carried Gus back to safety when his leg had been shot through and the rest of the company fled at White Oak Swamp.

"Well, damn her anyway," Corporal Wilson said. Wilson was a large, hard man, with a mean tongue, whom war had taught the need for occasional fairness. Gus could see through the shifting crowd of men—some of them shaking with the cold but unable to leave the body—that the corporal held a letter in his hand. "Just damn her all to Hell," he said. "Telling him how she went and married some worthless stay-at-home. And just before Christmas, damn her."

The captain returned then, from wherever captains go when duty pauses and the cold penetrates even the sturdiest, best-pitched tent.

"What's this now?" he demanded. "What's going on?"

The soldiers opened a path through their midst and the captain saw the boy sprawled, half in the tent and half out, with one foot bare and a fallen rifle beside him.

"Oh, Hell," the captain said.

"ASHES TO ASHES . . ." the preacher said. Gus had heard those words spoken so many times now, from hot Virginian camps to this dreary strip on the coast of the Carolinas, that he could have spoken them for himself. In English, too. The man of God added a warning of Divine surliness toward any other soldier who might even ponder such an act as Private Barrett had committed. The preacher had seen battles and he was hardened, and Gus was afraid he would show the dead boy no mercy. But the preacher softened toward the end and spoke of every human loss as a tragedy, even in the midst of a mighty war. Such a death was a loss for God, he said, as well as for his comrades.

"The birthday of Our Lord, Jesus Christ, is almost upon us," he concluded. "In this blessed season, let us renew the mercy in our hearts, and turn toward our fellow man in brotherhood and kindness. Amen."

The captain dismissed the company. The rumor was that the regimental colonel had lost his temper at the news, as he so often did nowadays, and wanted Private Barrett buried without ceremony, back of the dunes in an unmarked grave, as an example to the others. "Nothing but a worthless coward," the colonel was reported to have said. But Gus knew that the boy had been far from a coward. And if his wit had not been great, Billy Barrett's goodness had more than made up for the lack. So Gus had been glad to hear that the captain had threatened to resign his commission if he could not bury one of his own men as he saw fit.

The soldiers wandered off, less talkative than was their habit, and two Negroes began to shovel in the grave. Gus stood looking at the hole in the earth. The soil was little more than sand, and the lightness of it caught the wind and pinched his face with specks.

"*So eine Dummheit,*" he said to the vanishing coffin. "Such a foolish thing this is to do, Billy. Such a foolish thing . . ." And as there was no more drill that day and the war seemed to have gone to sleep for the winter, Gus wandered down toward the shore and watched other Negroes patrolling the line of the surf for washed-up treasures. They were everywhere now, the runaway slaves, begging for a nickel's worth of work or a meal, stealing sometimes, and Gus realized again how far the world had yet to go to achieve the dreams of his youth. He watched the waves and the figures in rags, and the dull horizon grew duller.

Gus spoke to the dead boy a final time. "You could have waited for my surprise. You should have waited, Billy. Only a little while."

WHEN GUS RETURNED to the camp, a half dozen men from his platoon were brewing coffee around a cooking fire. Corporal Wilson sat among them.

"Ain't he just the sorriest looking soldier in this army or any other?" the corporal asked before Gus could make it past. His voice longed to wound. "Hey, Dutch. What were you up to down by the water there?"

"*Nichts,*" Gus said. "Nothing. I am only thinking."

Corporal Wilson grinned. "I bet I know just what you were thinking, too." He looked around at the fire-warmed faces. "Know what old Gus was thinking, boys? He was looking on out over those waves and wishing he never crossed 'em. Wishing he was back over there in Dutch-land, with a big, fat gal to warm him up and no Rebels looking to put him out of his misery."

"Aw, let him be," Private McClean said, with a glance toward Gus. "He was friendly with Billy. Let him be for one day, at least."

The corporal twisted his mouth into a smile that pronounced his authority over others. "It's just every time I see him, old Dutch looks less like a soldier. I'm ashamed to turn out on parade with him." He accepted a pour of coffee from the communal pot. "Where you off to now, Dutchman?"

McClean lifted the pot toward Gus, offering him some, but Gus shook his head.

"I go over to the sutler now. To buy something, I think."

Corporal Wilson snickered. "Going to talk some Dutch with that damned Jew, ain't that right? I'd like to know what you and that fellow are up to. Probably Reb spies, the both of you."

"Bring me back a chaw, would you, Gus?" McClean asked. "I'll settle later."

As Gus walked off along the row of tents with their winter collars of wood, he heard the corporal say, "Yes, sir. Old Gus wishes he never had crossed that ocean down there. He's wishing he was back over there where life's all beer and sausages."

The corporal was wrong.

Gus knew he would never look like a picture-book soldier. He was short and far from handsome, and no amount of campaigning seemed to reduce the little lump of belly that stretched out his uniform. He recognized that he was not the sort of man who would inspire others on the field of battle. But he also had learned that he could make himself stand and fight when others ran away, as Corporal Wilson had run at White Oak Swamp, with a look of mortal terror in his eyes. And Gus knew, as well, that Wilson would never forgive him for seeing that look and for not running himself. As for wishing himself back in Germany, it was only the small things he missed now and then. He had never regretted coming to America, not for a single day, not even as he lay among the wounded in the Virginia barnyard that had served as a hospital. And though he did not believe that war was ever good, he had grown convinced that war was sometimes necessary.

Germany? His fatherland lay well behind him, a decade and more in the past. When he remembered Germany, he remembered the taunts at school, where his father had paid an extra fee to enroll him—money earned by a tailor's crippling work and killing hours. And he remembered the wonders the university had promised, and the reality of the treatment he had received from the students who wore the caps and colors of dueling societies and who were born to more wealth and power than other men could achieve in a lifetime. Gus recalled the vivid dreams of freedom, of the brotherhood of man, and all the golden words and the colossal, foolish hopes of 1848. It had seemed as though the German nation had thrown off its shackles at last. But they had all been nothing but fools. The powerful had deep roots, while the men on the barricades had none. He had fought to the end, though, long after others had given up, until the Prussian firing squads shot the last breath out of the revolution against the walls of Rastatt. He would have ended up among the bodies thrown into mass graves and forgotten, had a seller of second-hand clothes not hidden him in an attic.

A fugitive, he had come to America, to Cincinnati, which almost seemed a German city under the flood of emigration the failed revolution unleashed. And he had joined the learned societies that hoped, one day, to bring freedom and unity to Germany, and he raised his voice in a patriotic singing society. He taught dutifully—and well, he believed—at Professor Gerber's *Gymnasium und Lateinschule*. He even fell in love and hoped to marry, although his beloved disappointed him and chose a brewer.

Slowly, the dreams of liberating a distant homeland faded and the marvelous decencies of a new country charmed him. He had abandoned religion years before, deciding it oppressed and benumbed the people, but he believed in principles such as the Brotherhood of Man and the inevitability of human freedom, and even in certain doctrines of Socialism. Above all, he came to believe in the United States of America, where he doffed his hat to those whom he respected, not to those whose birthright made him small.

There were still nights when he read Heinrich Heine and grew wistful, but the nostalgia weakened with the years. He joined an abolitionist society and let his membership lapse in the organizations that looked backward, back across the ever-widening ocean. His parents died within months of each other, still in Frankfurt, and he mourned them but gained a deepened sense of freedom as his inheritance. The last ties had been severed. His home was on the Ohio River, not the Main or Rhine. When the war came, he embraced the Union's cause as if it were the bride he had never captured.

He did not join a German-speaking regiment, since orders barked in his native tongue brought back unbearable memories. Instead, he went up the river to Pittsburgh to enlist. At thirty-six, he had been the oldest volunteer in his company, and the others made fun of his accent and his slowness and the strains of gray in his beard, calling him "Gramps," or "Dumb Dutch," although he had a better education than any of the regimental officers. It was the tailor's skills, inherited from his father, that finally won him a small measure of acceptance, for a soldier's life is always stitched and patched. And as the jokes grew stale and dwindled, his comrades also learned that, even though he spoke with a foreign accent, his written English was as fine as his hand was fair. He wrote letters home for boys who, if they could write at all, scribbled in the awkward block letters of childhood. And he did it all with a good heart. Because these were his brothers now, whether they knew it or not, and they were all his fellow conspirators, as well, in a greater struggle than they seemed to know.

GUS FOUND THE sutler's wagon at the usual spot by the road that led to the landing. Two soldiers in overcoats and faded zouave trousers bargained over a wheel of cheese.

"That's a stinking lot of money for a cheese," a sergeant said. "I never paid that much money for a cheese in my life."

"From Philadelphia it has to come," the sutler told him. "With the boat. So there is more to pay."

"Oh, just give him the money, Charlie," the other soldier said. "You buy from a Jew, he's going to cheat you one way or the other."

The sutler knew enough to hold his tongue and let the transaction proceed. As the two soldiers ambled away, one drew a knife and cut yellow wedges for himself and his friend to eat.

"*Herr Professor!*" the merchant said with a smile, switching into his native tongue to speak to Gus. "It is always an honor! But today you look as sad as the young Werther . . ."

"Not quite that sad. It's only the weather," Gus said. "And how are you, *Herr* Rosen? How's business?"

The sutler shrugged and threw a look toward the heart of the camp. "If I give everything for free, I think I do the greatest business in the world." Then his bearded face took on a wistful look. "I tell you what I think, *Herr Professor*. I think the war should stop and all of them boys go home for this Christmas-time of theirs. I make money, oh, yes. They are lonely and think of the home, so they buy everything. Things they don't even want, they buy. Maybe they buy my wagon next. But I tell you what I think, *Herr Professor*: I make a bargain. Solomon Rosen gives up his profit from their Christmas if these boys can all go home." He laid his hand over his heart. "They're good boys. It hurts a man to see."

"Well, they can't go home," Gus said softly.

The merchant sighed and leaned back against his wagon. But he smiled a little, too. "Then I sell to them. What do you think, *Herr Professor*?"

"I think you'll be a rich man before this war is over," Gus said, wearing his first smile in days.

"From your lips to God's ear." The merchant held out empty hands. "At the moment . . ."

"At the moment, you can sell me a plug of chewing tobacco."

The sutler lifted an eyebrow. "He chews tobacco now? A professor? Like the boy from the farm?"

"It's for somebody else. Listen, *Herr* Rosen . . . I just want to be certain—"

"All is in order! Everything. All will be as you want. You have the word of Solomon Rosen, *Herr Professor*." The sutler smiled warmly. "If I am not being shot by these Rebels."

"Well, if you do get shot, do it afterward. Understand?" Gus paid for the plug of tobacco.

As he was about to leave, the sutler said, "You're a good man, *Herr Professor*. Too good to be a soldier, I think."

THAT NIGHT, GUS and his closest comrades sat around the stove as sleet matted the windward side of their tent.

"Ain't it queer," O'Dwyer said, "how you'll go losing a dozen in battle, and missing them every one, to be sure . . . but for Barrett to do what he did leaves your heart all bleeding?"

"I don't want to talk about it," Hendricks said. "Somebody sing us a song."

"He never stopped talking about her," McClean told them all. "I guess that was just bad luck. Seemed like that girl was all he ever thought about. Isn't that so, Gus?"

Yes, it was so. But Gus was wary of saying too much, or of saying the wrong thing. Because he knew that every man around the stove but him had a wife or sweetheart, and no matter the strength of the love and faith between each man and woman, the girl who had jilted Billy Barrett had loosed a ghost of doubt in each man's heart. And Gus, who had no love to worry over, never underestimated the force of loneliness.

"I think she is not a usual woman," Gus told them. "With the usual woman, I think the love becomes stronger when it is like this, with the separating."

"Well, I can't speak at all for the ladies," O'Dwyer said. "But if I'm not missing the old woman twicet what I ought, and pining for the terrible sight of her, there isn't a landlord left in all Ireland."

"I wish this war was over and done," Carpenter, the youngest of them, said.

"Somebody sing a Christmas song," Hendricks demanded. "Or just something happy, all right?"

"I don't feel like singing none," Carpenter said. "And I wish it wasn't Christmas coming, either. It just makes everything worse."

"Well, you wouldn't like Christmas in Mayo none the better," O'Dwyer said, "for it only means the black priests come round, squeezing every last penny out of a man. Last time, it was, I told Father Flannery, 'Father,' says I, 'here you're asking me to give charity to the poor, and I'm poor as the Baby Jaysus himself, so I'll tell you what I'll do, Father.' And I takes out the coins from my right pocket and jingles and jockeys them into my left before his very eyes, and I says, 'There, Father, I've saved you the time and the bother of transporting the silver, for I've given to the poor for all to see.' Oh, wasn't the old woman sore at me, and calling down all of the saints?"

"I suppose," Carpenter began, with his young eyes glowing as if a man's eyes could sweat, "a girl could go and forget a fellow. Just forget him. What he's like, I mean. And how it was when they was together . . ."

"They don't forget," McClean said, almost angrily. "Not the good ones. They don't forget any more than a man does."

"Women are weak. They're the weaker vessels," Hendricks insisted. Then he faltered and said, "I sure would like to hear somebody play on the fiddle, though."

"If I had a fiddle, I'd break it over your head," McClean told him.

"I've always liked a fiddle tune meself," O'Dwyer said.

"Hey, Gus," McClean called, in a changed voice that sought to change the mood, "You Germans like Christmas a lot, don't you? Don't Germans make a great big fuss about it? Even more than most folks?"

Gus nodded. But no words followed.

"Well, you're quiet tonight," McClean declared. "Wilson get to you again?"

"No," Gus said. "Only, sometimes the thoughts are so many that a man has nothing to say. Sometimes there are too many thoughts."

"I've always felt the same way meself," O'Dwyer agreed. "No sooner's a man blessed with a sliver of happiness, than worries come barking and biting him from behind. It's a terrible thing, a man's brain, just a terrible thing."

"I wish it wasn't Christmas," Carpenter said again.

"Well, it's not Christmas," McClean told him. "Not until the day after tomorrow."

"Won't nobody sing just one song?" Hendricks asked. "I feel so glum, I'd just like to hear one single song."

"*Camptown races sing dis song, doo-dah, doo-dah,*" O'Dwyer croaked. He had no voice and knew it, Irishman though he was.

"I will sing you a song," Gus said. "But it is in German only."

"I don't want to hear no German song," Hendricks said.

"You sing it," McClean told Gus. "I want to hear it. What's it about?"

"It is made from a poem. By the great poet Heinrich Heine, who loved freedom very much. But this is a song about the children only. It tells of the childhood that is gone now. How the heart breaks to think of it."

Gus stood up, as he would have done back in Cincinnati, where his had been one of the finest voices in the *Singverein*.

"*Mein Kind, wir waren Kinder . . . zwei Kinder klein und froh . . .*"

"Shut up over there," a voice shouted from an adjacent tent. "Can't a body get a little peace?"

THE DAY BEFORE Christmas dawned with water frozen in the buckets and pails outside the tents, but the sky promised to clear. Huge gray clouds raced in from the sea and blocked the sun, but they seemed to be fighting a rear-guard action against better weather following in pursuit. The air dried out, but remained cold.

Company drill was briefer than usual, and done a little carelessly. After announcing that General Foster had won a victory over at Kinston some days before, the captain told them that the company had not drawn any regimental or brigade duty until the day after Christmas, except the regular sentry posting, and, further, he was going to treat every man in the company to a Christmas Eve whisky after dinner. The men cheered him, and agreed that no company in the army had a finer captain.

There was still the company duty to be gotten through, and Gus and his platoon were detailed to gather firewood. They had been in the camp for weeks now, and had to go farther inland for each load of wood, and it was important to finish before dark, since the pickets had a habit of firing before they knew what they were firing at. At first, Negroes had brought in loads of wood to sell for a few pennies or trade for food or a little coffee, but the deliveries had stopped abruptly. When questioned, one of the older Negroes lingering about the camp said that seven of them had been shot down by Confederate rangers for bringing the wood in, and that the word had been spoken that the same would happen to any other Negroes helping out the Yankee army.

"They got more mean than they knows what to do with," the Negro had said. "Them pater-rollers got mean and to spare."

So the firewood details went out with rifles loaded, walking beside the mule-drawn wagon and watching the scrub for signs of a bushwhack. Close in, only the low pines remained, and they weren't worth the bother of cutting down, so the details edged ever deeper into the bleak countryside.

"I don't like it out here," Hendricks said. "Don't know why we don't just let the Rebs have it. Place ain't good for nothing."

"I don't know," McClean said. "I was thinking how, after the war, I might just come down here and buy myself one of those great big plantations."

"And from where would you be stealing the money to do that, your lordship?" O'Dwyer asked.

"You all be quiet," Corporal Wilson ordered. "No need to shout at the Rebs."

"Sure, and they can hear the squeak of that wagon two miles away," O'Dwyer said.

"Well, they don't need to hear your squeaking, too."

So the men walked in silence thereafter, into the hostile land, with the cold wind at their backs. Wafers of ice covered the puddles along the road and in the ditches, but the marshes looked wet and gray and dull. Feathers puffed out, birds watched the men from high branches, as quiet and still as if frozen.

"Wish I had me a turkey," Carpenter said. "Come Christmas, we always had us a turkey."

"I favor a ham meself," O'Dwyer responded, "but a turkey

would do me nicely. And a goose cooked proper makes the loveliest eating of all."

"Would all of you just shut up?" Hendricks begged.

"I wish it wasn't Christmas," Carpenter said.

"Well, try telling yourself it's the Fourth of July," Corporal Wilson said. Then he drew up. "Fair cutting over there, looks like."

With Hendricks and O'Dwyer—notoriously the least vigorous workers—standing guard with rifles at the ready, the rest of the men plodded into the marshland with their axes. At first, they were wary of the foreign world around them and sneaked looks into the undergrowth each time they paused for breath, but soon enough their work consumed them, the harvesting of fallen trees not yet rotted and the selection of others to be cut down and carried to the wagon.

"My damned feet are all wet," McClean said. He was a robust man, infinitely decent in Gus's experience, and he rarely complained. But no man was in good spirits now. The weight of the coming holiday bent their shoulders like the force of a cold rain.

When the work was done well enough to pass muster with any silly lieutenant who might have a mind to measure and count, the men put on the coats and jackets they had removed during their exertions and began walking back toward the wagon.

"Please. One minute, please," Gus said. He trailed off into the marsh with his axe over his shoulder.

"Where's Dutch going now?" Corporal Wilson called from the rear of the wagon, where he stood lighting up a cheroot.

"I'd better go with him," McClean told Carpenter. "You keep Wilson happy for a minute. God knows what old Gus is up to."

When McClean caught up with Gus, he found him chopping awkwardly at the base of an evergreen.

"What in the world . . ."

Gus paused, smiling. "See what a good tree? A *Tannenbaum*. Like my name. A good, straight tree."

"A sight bigger than you, though," McClean commented.

"There must be a Christmas tree," Gus said. "Before, I think we will only have one of those by the camp. Only they are not good. Not like this. I see this tree and think it is maybe the best."

"Wilson's going to give you Hell," McClean told him. He shook his head but unshouldered his own axe and told Gus to stand back.

As the two men approached the wagon with the tree, each of them expected Corporal Wilson to start hollering and cursing. But Wilson only said, "More Dutch nonsense" in a voice so dull it almost disappointed.

Carpenter was pleased, though. "We always had us a German tree back home," he said as he helped loft the pine atop the load of wood. "With candles. Lots of them."

And then the men began the cold walk back, into the wind, with the holiday sadness still pressing down upon them.

"THAT'S JUST THE dumbest thing I ever heard of," Corporal Wilson said, loud enough for many a man to hear. "Cutting down a perfectly good tree just to prop it up somewheres else. Leave it to your dumb Dutch to come up with something like that."

"I like a German tree," a man from the next platoon put in, as the little crowd watched Gus and McClean and Carpenter trying to brace the pine upright. "It always makes things seem kind of happy."

The wind was down, but Gus feared that the tree would topple over if not fixed just right. His heart was in the effort, and hearts do not reason, and it seemed as if it would be the worst thing in the world were the tree to fall over before morning. The early dark had covered the camp, and they had only the firelight to work by, but Gus was relentless. His energy was such that it swept up McClean and Carpenter, as well, and they worked through their soldier's dinner.

The captain appeared suddenly, re-emerging from the secret officers' world that swallowed him for hours at a time. Gus's heart thumped. He liked the captain, and believed he was a good man, but a fear coursed through him that the officer might find the tree a frivolity and unbecoming to military order.

The captain paused and folded his arms across his chest. "That's a fine idea," he announced. "It's a custom my wife won't do without, you know. Good work, men."

Gus felt as if the life of a child had been spared.

And then the draughts of whisky were drawn from a keg into each man's cup and someone produced a banjo. Half the company gathered to sing and, although the songs only made them lonelier, they made them feel better, too. For there is a little miracle in a song that will not be explained. They sang of home, and just a few songs of war, and then the Christmas hymns could be avoided no longer. The latter were rendered without accompaniment, since the banjo player could not follow their complexity, but specialized in the simple chords with which soldiers wet their eyes.

Carpenter brought a candle from his tent and tried to bind it to the tree, but could not make it stand up, since he lacked the proper fixture. So he settled in by the campfire, with a distant look in his eyes. The regimental chaplain stopped by the company on his rounds, reminding them all of the import of the coming night and suggesting that attendance at the next day's service was mandatory in the eyes of God, even if not required by the War Department's regulations. When he passed to another campfire, trailing blessings and rue, bottles came out of tents and pockets. But no one drank himself into a hard-ness. For a general sadness had cloaked the camp, and a veil of loneliness had fallen over each and every man, and a swig of whisky only made them weary. The night turned cold, and men drifted off for a last visit to the latrines or went directly to their tents, and the fire settled to a glow.

The last man by the embers was Gustave Tannenbaum, wrapped in his army overcoat and a knit scarf he had been given by a visiting delegation of the Sanitary Commission. The night was clear, if biting, and the heavens seemed an end-less celebration of stars. Gus had left religion behind long ago, on principle, because all superstitions slowed mankind's march to a better future. Yet, as the years whisked by, he had begun to see the human need behind the habits and customs that went along with faith. Holidays, for example, had a use-ful purpose. Men needed something to anticipate, to believe that exceptional events might occur in their humdrum, frag-ile lives. To believe that joy might not be denied them every single day of their existence. Gus had learned at the barrel of a gun that the holiday slogan of "Peace on earth, goodwill toward men" was hardly the stuff of mankind's daily practice. Whether or not there were omniscient spirits up there in the black spaces between those cold, white lights, a dose of good-ness, of simple kindness, had come to seem a harmless medi-cine to him.

"I'm getting old," he told himself, and felt the briefest pang at the thought of other men's good fortune in possessing families and mortal love to sustain them.

He poked the ashes with a stick. The warmth was no more than a ghost now. And then he sensed it was time, although the truth was that he had grown impatient and could sit still no longer. He rose and walked out to the edge of the tentage and a little beyond, whistling to make himself conspicuous in the darkness. For even though the internal sentries stood in little or no danger, the night discovered fears that day did not.

"Who's there?" a voice called.

"It's only me. Gus Tannenbaum."

"Well, what the devil are you up to, Dutch?" Gus recognized the voice and sloping shoulders of Cullen, a private from the first platoon.

"There is a surprise coming. Don't shoot, please."

"What kind of surprise? Does the captain know?"

"It's a good surprise," Gus said. "Wait now, and see."

The sutler was late and Gus began to worry that his endeavor would come to nothing. The thought was almost as crushing as Billy Barrett's death had been, for human beings feel a small present loss more deeply than yesterday's great one. He was near despair when he finally heard the jingle of harness and the creak of a hard-used wagon that wanted greasing.

"It's all right," Gus told the sentry. "Everything is in order. It's the sutler."

"The Jew fella?"

"Yes. He brings me something. For everybody. For everybody in the company."

"I don't know," Cullen said. "I don't want no trouble."

"No trouble," Gus said. And then *Herr* Rosen and his trap pulled up in front of them, suddenly distinct in the starlight, and there was no trouble because Cullen was not the sort of boy to shoot anybody, war or no war, and he let the wagon pass with all its treasures.

"Alles wie befohlen!" the sutler called. *"Ganz genau wie bestellt!* Everything you wish, *Herr Professor.* Even the *Stollen.* So much butter it takes! I think the woman who makes it is robbing me."

"Quiet," Gus hushed him. "They must all sleep now. I make a surprise for them."

The sutler shook his head and great beard in the darkness. "I think you make a great waste. A nothing you are paid, *Herr Professor.* How long to make so much money? A year? More?"

"What do I need with money?" Gus asked. "They're my friends."

"I think many of them are nobody's friends."

"Just show me what you've brought, *Herr* Rosen," Gus told him.

The sutler put a nosebag on his mule—an animal for which he had a great affection, as he had for almost every living thing—and began to unload his cargo under the light of the

stars. The effort made him happy, for he was an honest and in-
dustrious man, and he was proud of the ingenuity he had
shown in gathering hams and turkeys and pies, baked and sug-
ared Christmas cakes rolled just as they were in the Rhineland
or in Franconia, cookies thriftless in their use of butter or
spiced with ginger, bottles of schnapps, the finest coffee the
emporia of the Union had to offer, a regiment's worth of fresh
eggs, a pair of thick woolen stockings for every man in the
company, and five dozen small white candles, as well as the tin
holders to fix them to a tree.

"It's going to be like an honest-to-God Christmas," Private
Cullen said, in a voice that might have belonged to a child,
and Gus had to remind him that he was on sentry duty and
really ought to go back to his post.

Unburdened, thanked, and paid a last installment, the sutler turned back to his wagon. But before he mounted the seat
and turned the mule, he drew out a last package. It was
wrapped in brown paper and he held it out toward Gus.

"For you, *Herr Professor.* A gift."

"A Christmas gift, *Herr* Rosen? From you?"

The sutler shook his head adamantly. "Quiet, before God
hears you. No Christmas gift. Only something from my
brother's shop in Philadelphia."

"Thank you, *Herr* Rosen. I'm afraid . . . I have nothing to
give you in return."

"What kind of gift would that be? If Solomon Rosen expects a gift in return? Anyway, it's nothing. A rag. To keep the rest of you warm."

"The rest of me?"

But the sutler had turned away, muttering, as was his wont, about the careless, wasteful nature of the world. And he and his mule dissolved back into the darkness.

Gus had a great deal of work to do, but he took a moment to open the sutler's gift. Except for a few tokens given at his school in Cincinnati, he had not received a gift in a very long time. This one was a pair of woolen undergarments, of a wool so soft it begged to caress the skin. It made Gus pause, for he did not think of himself as much deserving.

Carefully, he wrapped up the package again and bent to his labors. First, he decorated the tree with the candles, as careful as the best civilian surgeon, terrified the pine might topple down. Then he nudged the campfire back to life, just enough to provide warmth for the baked goods and hams, to keep them from freezing while he kept his vigil. After he had been relieved from sentry duty, Cullen came by and offered to help, and Gus whispered little tasks to him and let the boy sneak a pair of cookies into his mouth.

WHEN THE FIRST men stumbled from their tents in the morning, the aroma of thick-brewed, bounteous coffee stunned them. You would have thought them shocked into paralysis by a surprise attack. And then they smelled the hams warming on the embers by the fire's edge, and the first men to greet the dawn saw the candlelit tree.

From the stupor and wonder of those first moments, the camp passed into an uproar. It was as if a pulse coursed through the tents, waking men with the promptness and dependability of a mechanical wonder. The rising tumult drew the captain from the white tent set apart, his hair stiff and wild with stale macassar, and he appeared bewildered when a sergeant hoary as the hills thrust a mug of coffee and a plate of cake into his hand.

"Merry Christmas, sir," Sergeant McGuire said, "and, by your leave, I'll wish ye all the blessings o' the day!"

Only the first dozen men realized that Gus was the sponsor of the bounty laid out before them. Those who came after simply thrust out their hands and helped themselves, with the simple greed of children. Even as Gus wandered from man to man, handing out the pairs of woolen stockings—almost thick enough to serve as boots—there was little sense in the company that the generosity flowed from him.

It was Corporal Wilson who changed that. He stood between the tree and a pack of soldiers ravishing a ham and cried for all the world, "Dutch! Is all this craziness your doings? You damned fool Dutchman!" But his voice was merry, and kind, and unexpected.

All the men stopped, just for a moment. Gus found he

could not speak or face them, so he simply wandered along, handing out socks.

But the men would not be satisfied with that, and they gave him a cheer that roused the regimental colonel from his port-laden slumber, and for a moment the old fellow imagined he was a spry lieutenant again, leading his men into the Mexican volleys at the gates of Molino del Rey.

But Gus did not want cheers, for they embarrassed him. He was a shy man, and perhaps that, as well as the prospect of con-siderable wealth, had turned the woman he adored away from his affections and thrust her into the brewer's brawny arms. He truly did not expect or want thanks. It was only that he felt sorry for these men, and loved them as best he could, as he had loved the boys he had taught, the boys whose names appeared bitterly often in the letters from his fellow schoolmasters now, boys who had fallen at Shiloh or Corinth, or who had succumbed to camp fevers. Gus really had not heard the malice in the jibes hurled in his direction as the months turned into years, but he always felt the other men in their common blue coats marching at his shoulders. They were his family now, and that was all.

It was a good day, that Christmas in the middle of the war. There was no need to turn to army rations, for there was hon-est food enough to fill each belly twice and a little more. Men from other companies wandered by as the day progressed, dis-covering ties of friendship they had barely noticed before, and the regimental colonel, come round to deliver a Christmas address to the men, was persuaded, instead, to have a piece of pie, and then a second helping. He told the captain it was a grand thing, the way he had provided for his men, and that was the way an officer *should* behave. "Always take care of the men," he said between mouthfuls, and he hinted that a promotion might be in the wind. He would not listen when the captain, who was an honest man despite his rank, tried to explain that a private was responsible for the feast, for the colonel had served in the old army, in which colonels did the talking and captains and lieutenants did the listening.

Gus received attention enough, and more than he wanted, really. All of the men agreed that the Germans really knew how to celebrate Christmas, and Corporal Wilson admitted, with a sheepish look at Gus, that his wife was a Lutheran herself, although High German, of course, and not Low Dutch. And when the schnapps had gone around in the waning afternoon, and the men had time to think of distant hearts again, they grew sentimental and sang.

McClean called for Dutch to give them a German Christmas carol, and a chorus of voices seconded the request. Gus did his best to oblige. He had heard them often enough, those old songs. He began with *"Es ist ein' Ros' entsprungen,"* and he was in fine, clear voice that day, so he sang two more. The truth was that he knew only a smattering of the words, for the songs were not really his, but he threw bits of Heine into the gaps or simply made up rhymes. On that day, at least, the difference in language was an advantage, for the men listened raptly as he mouthed the nonsense lyrics, since he did it in such a lovely, haunting voice.

And when the camp settled down to sleep, Gus fell into his blankets in happy exhaustion. There were many things his comrades did not know about him, of course, not least that he had been born a Jew. He had never celebrated Christmas and felt no slightest tie to the Christian faith. His deeds that day were simple acts of kindness, his giving for the good of other men. He still had no use for any religion at that time in his life, although, after the war, he would marry a banker's plain, clear-thinking daughter and embrace the faith of his ancestors with all the devotion and vigor of a prodigal son returned. He would die respected, beloved and very old, surrounded by family and friends, as good a man as any in Cincinnati.

But Gus could not know any of those things that night, nor did he care. It mattered only that he had made his comrades happy, and for that one fine day they had all been brothers. If he did not share their faith, he shared the sentiment of "Peace on earth, goodwill toward men," and that was enough.

Nothing but a Kindness

ATTY HAWKS DIDN'T need two eyes to find his way up the trace to the house. Didn't even need one, to tell the truth. No night, not this one or any other, was dark enough to lead him astray now. The soles of his feet knew every rock bumping up through the packed earth, and the muscles in his legs held a memory of each change in the rise of the path, of every turning, a recollection that even death wouldn't burn away. He didn't need two eyes, or even the one left him. Still, he watched up ahead as he went. With a fierceness and a hunger in him. Aching for the first sign of home.

It was cold. The widow woman over in Dempsey who had boiled his uniform in a kettle to kill whatever had taken to calling it home had given him an old black overcoat, but there was enough temper to this cold to keep him shivering as he walked and climbed. It wasn't near as cold as it had been in the prison up in New York, nothing like that kind of cold, but it was cold enough. He drove his tired legs up the mountainside, with patches of snow down in the hollows like bandages on a wounded earth, and he shivered and watched for home, long before he had any chance to see it.

He was a lucky man. He knew that, though his luck troubled him. He had forced himself to remember that luck when the major with the white beard gave them a welcome-home speech with no caring in it at all, no understanding of how men were. Then the major had his clerks just turn loose all those who weren't fit for the army anymore, giving them stamped papers saying they were discharged and weren't deserters, handing those papers over without even looking up at the men standing before them. Natty Hawks hadn't expected bugles and drums. But there was a hasty feel to it all, an embarrassment in the face of men with parts gone missing, a plain-as-day wish to just be shut of them, that left him with an edge of sickness.

He was no use anymore. That was it. He was a man of no use to them. Didn't matter what he'd done. Or even that he'd had his fill of war and everything that went along with it. It was only that, after all the fighting and then the prison up there in Elmira, where the ladies and gentlemen of the town would climb up on platforms to look over the walls at them like they were all animals in a pen, starving, dying animals, after all that, he was no use to them.

At least he'd got the lice out of his hair. He believed he'd got rid of all of them now. And he never did get the camp itch. He'd dreaded it, but never got it. Haunted by the way men scratched themselves bloody, raw as a skinned carcass, and nothing anybody could do about it. With the Yankee soldiers just mean-eyed up there in the guard towers, just killing mean. Men froze to death, or coughed themselves to death, and the Yankees just counted one less ration for each one gone. Not that the rations were much.

Natty Hawks went up the trail, running in fits then slowing again, aching in that place between all that's gone but still crying to be felt and the things still coming toward a man. He just wanted to be home. Just that.

It struck him how quiet things were on the mountainside. He had almost forgotten that kind of quiet. It suited Christmas Eve. And it suited home. He hadn't known this kind of quiet, an almost-pure silence, in a long time. It was never quiet in the army, not even in the dead of night, when nightmares made men cry out in the deep loneliness of sleep, while others just snored or wheezed and horses shifted and neighed, as if beasts had dreams of their own. And fighting, when it came, was the noisiest thing on God's green earth. But even that was better than the sounds of the prison, a noise that was just one endless, terrible complaint, cursing by day and coughing by night, and dying all the time. The noise your insides made when you were hungry. And the calling-out that went with fever dreams. Or the laughter of the well-fed men out past the fence-line.

And then he saw the glimmer up the mountainside, the yellow hint of firelight spilling out through shutters. It wasn't moonlight, not that frosty paleness, nor a reflection of the sort that gave a man's hiding place away and let you see an ambush a few seconds before it happened. It was the light of home.

That would be Old-Ma sitting up. Dozing by now, might be, given the lateness. Old-Ma sitting in her rocker by the fire, wrapped up in the coat that had belonged to Old-Pa, so long ago that those times were hardly a memory, a thick-set woman shrinking with the years, everything about her shrinking but her heart. And that heart was as large as the mountain. Larger. Her whole life was nothing but a kindness.

It warmed him, just the thought, and lifted his feet as surely as it lifted his spirits. He knew he was home then, really home, and that all the rest of it was done now. Because Old Ma would be sitting there, maybe sleeping in her rocker, or maybe still working through a chapter in the Bible that had come to belong to her as surely as her hands and feet did, a Bible marked and turned down and spotted with decades of touching every single page. And she lived that way, if nobody else in the world did, nobody but her. She lived a Christian woman's life so that it didn't even seem like there was any trying in it, as if it had been born into her, as if her kindness was natural as breathing. On those days when his father's hard face eased a little, he was fond of saying that Old-Ma would've fixed a plate for Judas Iscariot, if he ever came by, and prayed him along on his travels.

His father. Morning would be time enough for that.

The house shaped itself out of the moonlight, built over and around the cabin Old-Pa had put up in the years before there was anybody called Hawks on the mountain except him and Old-Ma. When man and wife weren't old anything and Indians still came over the trace, though mostly just wandering from nowhere to nowhere by then. Natty could see the second story put up with boards and the side wings that had grown on, and the barn looming over in the swale. All quiet, as if it had been frozen the day he left and kept just like that, waiting for him.

He went up the house path with things tumbling over inside of him and he listened to his own footfalls on the planks of the front porch.

He let himself in. Still no lock on that door, war or not. Maybe it was time to put one on, given things he'd heard down in the valley.

Then he saw her.

She was sitting there, but she wasn't asleep. It was as if she had been waiting for him. Heard him coming when he was still hours away. Still days and weeks away. And she looked just the same as ever.

Old-Ma smiled at him, a smile that was better than rising

and wrapping him in her arms, better than just about anything at all. And she put a finger to her lips to hush him.

He set his sack of nothing down by the door and went to her. She held up her arms then, and though the fire was down to the embers, it was as if he could see right through the big sleeves of that coat to what little was left of the arms that had cradled him and his brothers and sisters in turn.

A man might forget a lot in life. But not those eyes. Blue as good water.

He bent down to let her reach him without any more effort and he kissed her cheek. It was cold-skinned, the way old folks are, as if the heat of life pulled back inside them with the years. Her cheeks were thinned to looking through.

"Natty," she said. "I knew you'd come home all right. I knew that. That's all right, now. You cry if you want to. Nothing wrong with it. Just hush and let folks sleep. And let's us two visit."

She shifted the Bible in her lap and looked at him. Not at the leather patch that covered the emptiness where his right eye had been. She didn't seem to take the least interest in that. She looked at him like he was six years old again. He was as welcome as that.

"Old-Ma," he said. "Old-Ma."

"You sit down now. And let's us visit. It's all right, now."

And he hadn't expected anything like this, hadn't known there was all this weakness and sorrow in him, just waiting to burst out. He couldn't say anything at all for a time, just sat bent over in a straight-back chair and wept. She watched him as if it was the most natural thing in the world for a man to cry like that.

"It's all right, now," she whispered after a time. "You're home."

"I didn't know," he said at last, keeping his voice down. He had enough of a hold over himself to know that he didn't want the rest of the family to wake and come out to him, not yet. He just wanted this time to sit and learn how to be decent again. With Old-Ma, who never knew how to be anything but decent. "I didn't know what it was going to be like," he continued. "I didn't know I could be like that. Nor any man."

His grandmother just smiled on, with lips that had no color anymore but the color memories painted on them.

"I done things," he said, "that won't let me be. I can't tell you what it's like. The hating that fills you right up. You get all caught up in things, and you hate men you don't even know— men you're never going to know—and you kill them like they're no better than squirrels. It makes you happy in a way you don't want to feel. It makes you happier than most any-thing, long as you're doing it. I done things for my pleasure that the Devil wouldn't do in Hell."

Old-Ma patted the Bible. "It's all in here, Natty. Jesus knows. The Lord knows all about those things. It's all been told. First the deed, and then the sorrow. If the repentance is true, a healing comes after."

"I don't know if it's sorrow, Old-Ma. Or if I'm just scared of how I am."

"The fear of the Lord is the beginning of wisdom," she said. "There's nothing can't be forgiven a true heart."

"I don't know if I have a true heart," Natty told her.

She smiled that endless smile. "We'll pray over that."

"It's just," he began, with his voice wavering like a line about to break and retreat, "it's just that there was so much dying. It stopped seeming important. I took to liking what they handed me to do. I *liked* killing those men, Old-Ma. And I would've gone on killing them until they killed me or there were none of them left, if Colonel Massey hadn't surrendered us. Just up and surrendered us, to save his own skin. Just gave us all up, after we fought for him. After we trusted him."

The fire sparked. For the first time, Natty sensed its warmth, the low, even warmth that comes from the last core of good, hard wood. Until then, all the warmth had come from his grandmother, so it seemed. All the warmth he needed, anyway.

"Well," she said, in the weathered voice time had left her, "maybe that was for the best, now. Him giving you boys up. To stop you from any more killing."

"He gave us up to save his own skin."

"Well, now, maybe it was for the best, anyways."

He looked over at the tiny figure swaddled in the big coat. His memories of her were a thickness in him, a dense goodness of details grown together until all the past was present at once.

"How could it be for the best?" he asked her, as if she truly might know. "When it only meant they penned us up like sheep not even worth the slaughtering. Penned us up and starved us slow. Froze us. And laughed at us all the while." He shook his head in a sorrow nothing would ever measure. "You don't know what men will do in a prison like that. The things I done myself." He fixed his wet eyes on her. "And then they let me go on the exchange. Me, alone, of the five of us left close. Me, and not thirty others out of the scraps of the whole regiment. And I was glad, Old-Ma. I didn't care a lick about anybody left behind. Not as long as I was picked to go."

"Most like, they let you go," she said, "because of your eye there. Because you ain't going to do no more shooting without that eye. The Lord took from you the instrument of evil, and then he gave you another chance."

And it was strange to hear her say that, because there was a trueness in it. The Yankees had sent back men missing arms or legs, men addled in the head from all they'd seen, men whose hands were fingerless paws, whether or not they were on the exchange list. When they finally got back South, not half of the names had matched.

"I left better men than me back there," he said softly, with humility as real and incontestable as the blade of a plow was hard.

"You just try to be the best man you can," Old-Ma told him. "I know you'll do that now. And the Lord will decide who's the first and who's the last."

They sat for a time. Then he added a single log to the fire. Not enough to disturb the feeling of the house or wake anyone else. Just enough to warm them a little more and light them a little longer.

"I guess it's Christmas morning by now," he said.

Her lips parted, but her smile did not fade. "Long since, I expect. Merry Christmas, Natty."

"Merry Christmas, Old-Ma. How's Mama?"

His grandmother nodded. "Better, I think. Better than when you left. Not that she didn't cry for a time. But she's come to see her way through things a sight better. I think the Lord's shown her the way."

"And everybody else? How's Becky?"

The smile did not fade, although Old-Ma said, "It's been hard on her. Lonnie Coleman was killed a time back. Word didn't come right away, with him up there on the Union side. Becky fell into a sorrow, though she's picking up of late."

"I didn't know."

"Of course, you didn't."

Natty twisted his mouth and looked at the fire. "I guess Pa would've had me killed and Lonnie come back, if they'd handed him the choosing."

Her admonishment was soft, but piercing. "Don't say that,

now. You know it isn't true. You'll never be a good man, or any kind of man, if you say things like that. That's all pity on yourself and no sense."

"I only meant him going with the Yankees. Pa liked that well enough."

"You didn't ask about your Pa, Natty."

"How is he?"

"Well. He's well enough. He'll be pleased to see you. More pleased than he'll show. He'll be well-pleased."

"He'll never forgive me."

"That's silly talk. And just more pity on yourself. Stop that now. And you listen to me. The war's changed more things than just you. Oh, your Pa's still a Union man, and I expect he always will be. If I cared about things like that, I expect I might declare myself a Union woman, like most folks this side of the mountain. And how could he not be angered, Natty? Seeing you go off to serve under the man who took his land? Who took away the land Old-Pa claimed and cleared before him? Your Pa's a hurt and disappointed man, a man who's had wrong done to him and can't do nothing about it. It tells on a man and his pride, even more than getting herself hurt and disappointed tells on a woman." She straightened her shoulders a touch. "You expect too much of your Pa and too little of yourself sometimes."

He winced. "Pa didn't understand any bit of it. Not any bit. North or South, Union or Confederate, none of that mattered, Old-Ma. It was only that all my friends were going for the South, and I couldn't go against them." He smiled, bitter as dug-up roots. "We figured it was going to be as much of a good time as a man could have on this earth. That's all. I just went with my friends. I couldn't go with the Yankees and go against my friends. That's all."

"Natty? I want you to promise me something. For my Christmas. I want you to promise me you'll go slow with your Pa. That you'll give him time. In his heart, he'll be overflowing when he sees you. Just overflowing. Like a man set free of Babylon and looking on over into Canaan from a mountaintop. But it's hard for him to show things like that. As hard as it is for you to keep your temper. I want you to promise me you'll just love your Pa, whatever comes. Promise me, now."

He closed his eyes and summoned the strength left to him. "I promise." He tried to mean it. For her. For Old-Ma.

She held up the Bible. Holding it up just a little way. With both hands. Shaking. It wounded him to see how weak she was now.

He came to her and knelt down, and placed his hand on the Book.

"I swear," he said.

"That's right. You keep the promise, and everything's going to come right. You just keep your promise." She smiled. "They're all going to be so happy to see you. You don't know. You haven't lived long enough to know."

"I've seen more than you think," he said.

"That's pride talking now," she told him. "Oh, Natty. It's going to be just fine. That's what it's all going to be. You'll see."

He didn't understand her, of course. "I heard there's been fighting in the valley. That folks are turning mean on each other. With the Yankees coming and going."

"The things that matter are going to be fine. I wasn't talking about the things of this earth. Not the outward things. Only the love." She rocked a bit. "You remember the story of the prodigal son? Surely, you do."

He nodded.

"Well, that's your story. Oh, don't make faces. To your pa, that's who you are. Even if you think you're Moses himself, come to lead the people to the Promised Land. Or Royal David."

"I don't think that."

"No. I suppose not. I'm just an old woman, and I'm tired. And I'm not talking any more clear than I'm thinking, I suppose. I'm so tired." She yawned, a tiny gesture of the mouth, a slight arch of the neck. "But I'll tell you this one thing, and you remember it. You can't go wrong by loving. Even if a man loves a bad woman, or a woman a bad man. Even if you love a body who betrays you for thirty pieces of silver. Or for a sight less than that. If you love, if you just love and don't stop loving, everything comes right."

He could not believe that. He had seen too much hatred. And he had seen love twisted and torn until it was a mockery. Love had come to seem as thin and fragile and useless as wet cartridge paper. Not his grandmother's love, but that was special. There was no other love like that left in the world. Not even his ma loved like that, with her worn-down face and her temper that turned into days of crying. Love was the rarest thing on this earth.

"You're tired now," Old-Ma said. "You just set on back and rest a bit. You'll have the children crawling all over you soon enough, and you won't get any rest for days. You just set back and rest. And I'll do the same. You're home now, Natty. And everything's going to be all right."

As soon as she spoke those words, he felt how true they were. In a way he could not begin to describe. The way you just know a thing all of a sudden, then know it forever, from that day on.

He was tired. She was right about that, too. He had years of tired in him, all coming over him at once. It seemed to him he never had been this tired before, not after the hardest days of marching, or even in the time after a battle that was like a blackness in the soul, after all the spunk faded away and something deep inside you sensed what you had done. He closed his eyes, shutting them slowly, with Old-Ma's blue eyes upon him as he drowsed.

"Sleep now," she said.

LITTLE GABE WOKE him up with a holler. Eye-patch, beard and whatever else might have changed about him, Little Gabe saw right through it all and shouted, "Natty's home, Natty's come home for Christmas!"

They came tumbling downstairs and out of backrooms after that, eight children, from Carrie, who had changed so much he wouldn't have recognized her anywhere else but in the swarming, warm-smell pack of them, up to Becky, who had grown comely as the Rose of Sharon.

His mother came out then, with that hurt look of hers that was as constant as a favored garment, but she hugged him so hard he could feel her heart beating against him.

"I never known such a good Christmas," she told him.

Finally, his father came into the room, dressed, and walking slow as a man wary of danger. He stopped to have a look at his son from a distance. At the scrap of leather over one eye. And he waited there across the room, face changeable as a sky that could turn either way, to rain or sun, to light or darkness.

The house had fallen silent. As silent as the mountainside had been in the darkness of the night.

"Pa?" Natty said. "Am I welcome?"

As slowly as if the mountain itself were moving, his father nodded. Then he looked away and said, in a voice not half so strong as intended, "Sarah, I'll be round the back there. Call out when the coffee's boiled."

"You need help with anything, Pa?" Natty asked.

His father looked at him again, but could not sustain the

gaze. His eyes had turned weak. "I reckon I could use a hand," he said.

But before father and son went out into that Christmas morning, the empty rocking chair caught Natty's eye.

"Where's Old-Ma?" he asked the room full of family. "She still sleeping?"

The silence swelled back up.

His father, waiting by the door, spoke brusquely, though the strength in his voice rang false. "Old-Ma died last harvest time," he said. "She's gone."

But Natty's mother came to him and laid her arm around his waist. "Old-Ma knew how you loved her," she told her returned son. "Just about the last thing she said was that we weren't to worry, that you'd come back all right."

Christmas Gift

THE YANKEES CAME just before Christmas. Tied their horses to the fence like the place belonged to them and didn't even draw their pistols, just went on into the high house on their business. The Yankees had got used to winning. Everybody knew that. So they didn't expect no fuss from any Southerns. No, sir.

What few fighting men still showed themselves around the back country looked all beat down and unwilling, and that surely was a thing to see. Last time an acquaintance of the high house came by to tip his hat to Miss' Emily and water up his men's horses, you could tell those boys felt all beat down and worried. Looking back over their shoulders like black folk lying out somewheres. After them being so high and proud all the time. Just beat down and dirty and scared, every one of them. Jump at the barking of a dog.

The Yankees weren't that way at all. Dundee watched them from the barn door. They just went on into the house and started breaking things up. Dundee could hear them. Miss' Emily and the girl didn't say nothing to them, either. Didn't holler or start in to begging or crying. Miss' Emily was all cried out a ways back and now all she did was watch things go by like a penned cow. And the girl had never been right, anyway. Everybody knew that.

The Yankees had their own kind of meanness. Not like the hot, come-all-sudden meanness that slipped over the white men Dundee had known. Yankees weren't the whipping kind any more than they seemed the praying kind. Just went at things mean and quiet, though they liked to cause a damage. You could hear that much from the doing inside the house.

It struck Dundee that Southern white folks liked to get a hold of things just so they could throw them in each other's faces, just throw them all away like nothing mattered and go strutting around high and mighty on the strength of it. Yankees liked to get things and keep them all to themselves. Neither way of doing seemed Christian.

Most of the black folk had run off into the grove when the Yankees rode up. Honeymine went, too, soon as Dundee told her to git, because that woman knew when to listen and lay her temper aside. A few of the worthless sort went on forward to the fence and dawdled by the Yankee horses, waiting to see if any good luck might come to them. But the Lincoln soldiers didn't hardly see them, just pushed on past into the house and started in to doing. Dundee stayed on by the barn, saddle-soaping lines to keep them supple and all the while smelling the good leather smell in the cold. And watching. Dundee had spent a lifetime learning how to watch things. Often-times, a man did best to bide his time and see.

A worth of shouting rose up after a while, with a Yankee voice hollering at Miss' Emily and wanting to know where things was hid and did she want her house burned down around her? Dundee didn't hear Miss' Emily at all, for she'd just about given up on talking, and likely that just made the Yankee madder. He cursed her hard, but at least there wasn't no killing in his voice. Just a lack of getting what he wanted.

That eased Dundee's mind. He didn't believe he wanted to see any more harm done to Miss' Emily and the girl. Because he didn't know what he'd do then, if he heard them start in to screaming or crying that way. He didn't know what he'd do, but he feared it. Fearing the meanness stewing in himself. Might not do nothing at all, that was what troubled him as a Christian man. Might just let them be. Just let them see how bad things could turn. Just walk on away.

He could not drive the bitterness from his heart, the sharpness that he felt toward them, the Lord knew that too well, and sometimes what he felt seemed even worse than bitterness or sharpness, but he didn't want no hurt done to them, anyway. For fear of the Devil in his own heart, the Devil that made his heart beat stronger to see the mighty fallen. Afraid their suffering might please him. As it had pleased him before.

Some things were right, and some things were wrong. Other things weren't clear, though. A man didn't always feel what he wanted to feel.

He prayed for them, anyway. Praying against himself.

The hollering Yankee came down off the back porch, with all those fancy gold stripes up and down his arm and the other men following him. He looked about as happy as the gray sky hanging overhead. Ready to rain down vinegar.

The stripe-armed Yankee came over to Dundee. Another bluecoat fellow kept him company. The rest split up and went on into the barn or broke into the musty emptiness of the smokehouse.

Things you look at on a man are his eyes and his hands. The Yankee's eyes had a meanness, all right, but not the hardness you had to worry over. And his hands were almost rough as a fieldworker's. Man with hands like that been beaten down plenty of times himself, Dundee figured. Just go careful with a man like that and you wouldn't meet no big trouble. Just don't make him out to be small.

Dundee put down the lines and rose to show respect. Show that much respect was only sense and didn't cost nothing.

"You're free now, boy," the Yankee said, looking up at his face. "You ain't a slave no more."

"No, sir."

"No more whippings. You're free as a bird."

"Yes, sir. Like you say."

"So you owe us a debt. For freeing you."

Dundee canted his head and tensed, though not so the Yankee would notice.

"I want you to tell us where the lady of the house buried her silver. Her jewelry. Anything she's hiding."

"Ain't no silver, marse. Jewelry, neither. All that long gone. Little there was."

The Yankee stepped closer and cinched up his belt. "Don't sass me, boy. Don't you play me for a fool. You owe me an answer. You tell us where that witch hid whatever she had to hide, and we'll give you some of it for yourself. You can go off wherever you want. Get drunk for a month. She bury it? Or hide it somewheres?"

"Only thing Miss' Emily got to hide," Dundee said honestly, "is how she got nothing to go hiding. Everybody knows she's poor as white trash herself. Everybody says how it's a shame, marse. Just got that house there left to her. And the no-good acres. Nothing else. Everybody knows that."

"Well," the Yankee said, "she might not have that house much longer, either." He rested a hand on his holster. "I'm not sure you don't need yourself a lesson, boy. Why, I bet you're the head nigger. Looks like the head nigger, don't he, Jim? I bet you know a damned sight more than you're telling."

The second man edged closer. "Oh, let him be, Ike. Like as not, he's telling the truth. You saw the rags she had on. And that little girl."

"House like that," the stripe-armed man said, gesturing back toward the porch, "you know they got something to hide. Probably put on old clothes to fool us. Left things all dirty like that. I think this nigger needs a good talking to."

"He don't know nothing, Ike. For God's sake, just look at him. Dumb as a monkey. Let's move on. There's plenty to pick through down the road."

"I still think he's lying," the first Yankee said. "He's the big chief nigger, that's who he is. Who knows what goes on in that house while the men are off to war?" But he turned away and spat on the ground and headed for the pump. When the other men sauntered over to report that the place looked like it had been picked clean two times over, Stripe Arm shook his head in disgust and made to go. But before he did, he cast a look back at Dundee and said, "You're free now, boy. Liar or not. Merry Christmas from Billy Sherman and the Indiana cavalry."

DUNDEE HAD NOT lied. Not a bit. Wasn't a thing buried or hid that he knew of. Marse George had been a gambling man, not a working one. Didn't take no war to bring him down low and poor. Dundee knew his own age, and that was thirty-seven, and he had lived every one of those years on the place. *San Souci.* "San-soosey," how it was said. Old Marse Cutter had done fair for himself, but it didn't take young Marse George long to run things down and start in to selling off land and black folk, one after the other. Folks said as Miss' Emily didn't come with much and what did come along with her didn't last. Marse George had a fondness for Charleston and a high tone, though he always said Savannah never hurt him, neither.

Sold off Dundee's brother and his wife and two children all to a Mississippi trader come through leading a string he bought up in Virginia, and no crying or pleading wouldn't help. "Necessity rules all the earth," Marse George said. And he sold more black folks, too, although he never sold off Honeymine, thank the Lord, because she didn't breed and no white man was going to pay his money to buy a black woman who didn't breed, not if she wasn't young and handsome anymore, not if she wore a scar down her face like that. Dundee could bear a lot, he knew, for Man's lot was tribulation. But he didn't believe he could bear the loss of Honeymine. He feared he would not turn the other cheek, that he would strike the first blow. So God, in his wisdom, had made her fruitlessness a blessing. And spared them the suffering of the children might have been.

There was plenty fighting and suffering in the high house

long before any war came along, and Miss' Emily took on the permanent bitters after the child. Little Miss Polly. Never was right. Everybody knew that. And there was something of a blame to it, with Miss' Emily forgetting herself and screaming at Marse George about his doings in Charleston for all to hear and how the Lord was punishing them both and she was all sick inside. When the war did come, Marse George acted happy as a man who found a bag full of dollars under his bed and went off and got himself killed soon as he could at a place called Malvern Hill. Miss' Emily's two brothers had the same streak of luck themselves, one of them taken by the typhoid when he came home to visit, all pretty and stepping in his uniform, and the other shot to pieces at Iuka out west there. Miss' Emily tried to sell off more land to raise some keep-up money, but Honeymine heard tell how the townfolks wouldn't let her because the bank had papers on everything already and Miss' Emily couldn't do nothing at all, almost like she was made a slave herself.

Dundee did what had to be done. It was hard feeling even Christian charity toward Miss' Emily and the girl, for she had been proud in her days of glory, and cruel, but he did what had to be done. Because he could not stand to see a field go bad or an arm stay idle. When Honeymine read the Holy Bible to him nights, he understood this and that, but not all things. One thing worked through into a clearness, though. Every man was obliged to do his labor in the vineyards of the Lord.

And Dundee figured that, as there weren't any vineyards he knew of anywhere in the low-country, cotton rows, peas and sweet corn would do. Growing things made sense, even when men didn't. And black folks had to eat as well as white folks. It angered him when a body just leaned back and expected dinner to fall out of the sky like manna. And it didn't rain biscuits and bacon grease, either. Let the white folks fight and see what came of it. Meanwhile, just make sure that something was always sitting on the holding shelf for dinner.

Some of the slaves went off early on, soon as they could muster themselves. Others drifted off after they heard about Atlanta burned down like a judgement of the Last Days. Most waited to see and did what Dundee told them, more or less. Men didn't have to like the things they knew to cling to them. Dundee understood that. So he saw that the planting was done, and the husbanding, as Marse George always called it, and the harvesting, killing, rendering and the plowing when the time came around again. Everybody had something in the pot, though it never was like the good feeding days under Old Marse Cutter again. Better thick water than thin in the bowl.

And Dundee took the cotton into town, though it was hardly worth hitching the mules for what little it fetched nowadays, and all the prideful coloreds, all those who had been caught by the vanity of the world and its temptations, laughed and started in to woofing about how even a nigger wasn't poor as Miss' Emily Cutter, and if Dundee muled under folks that poor, what did that make him now? Mr. Walker, fellow owned the gin and bank both, and more besides, always looked at Dundee like he was looking over a horse he was fixing to buy.

Then, on a cool, gray morning a little before Christmas, the Yankees came. Before they left, they set Miss' Emily's house on fire, but it started raining hard right after that and the house only burned part way.

DUNDEE WENT BACK up to the high house after the rain stopped and before dark came. Miss' Emily didn't ever light the lamps or candles now. She just sat there in the dark with the girl. So Dundee went up while there was still a grayness like worn-through flannel in the air, to see if any real harm had been done.

The Yankees had busted what they could and turned the rest upside down. The hallway already had night in it and Dundee had to step careful. Smoke wandered through the rooms like haunts, heavy as grease on the skin and bitter sharp in the nose. Even so, even with all that smoke, he could smell how the house was dirty in the worst way. White or colored, no folks should live like that. It reeked to a turning.

Miss' Emily sat in the visiting parlor with the girl. Everything was ripped up and tore down and broke. She sat in a chair that had been cut with a knife and that Polly curled

against her legs how a dog does, or a fed cat. Dirty-cloth light
fell in through the big windows now that the coverings were
pulled down or hanging sideways. Miss' Emily just sat there
like she didn't see, though her eyes were bright. Brighter than
the light through the windows. Bright as fever.

The girl smiled up at him. Her nose needed cleaning off.

Fire was long out and Dundee got it started again. There
were still logs left by the fireplace, too many of them left. It
was days now since he had Rome take up a carry of wood. He
wondered how long the woman and the girl had gone without
warmth, and told himself he should've kept an eye on the
main chimney. The mighty have fallen, he thought, with a
meanness that pleased one side of him even as it shamed the
other.

When the bark on the logs caught he stood up and straightened his back. Darkness was creeping all through the room
and he wasn't going to be in any room with a white woman
after dark. Riders might come back, and not the Yankees.
Young ones, those as hadn't been to the war proper, had a
taste for killing black men these days. Since they couldn't kill
them any Yankees, Dundee thought bitterly. Remembering
how they shot down the Reverend Mr. Jeremiah. Shot him
down for speaking Scripture to them. Saying God didn't have
no niggers in mind.

"Miss' Emily," Dundee said, in a voice made soft, as if his
words were for the child not the woman, "you got to keep logs

on that fire there yourself. You got to do it yourself. It's cold now."

The woman turned her firelit eyes toward him, flooding the room with their venom.

"It's all your fault," she said. "You people. It's all your fault."

DAY BEFORE CHRISTMAS, Mr. Walker rode up in a buggy that used to sit in Marse George's barn. 'Til some time after the Malvern Hill news came through. Horse came from elsewheres. Fine one, too.

Dundee was back in the grove with Rome and two shovels, uncovering enough pots and tarpaulined bags to feed them all through a day or two. Honeymine ran to fetch him, running to make that welt down across her face hot purple and gleaming, and he left her there to watch Rome and "help." Rome was a good man. But he was a hungry man, too. Like every child of God among them.

Dundee took to cleaning out the chicken coop, which wasn't his work. But it did a man good to humble himself. The Holy Bible made that plain. And it brought him close enough to the high house to feel things going by. Fool's work, though. Hadn't been any chickens for months, and weren't like to be any. Only the stocks he buried soon as the crops were in and rendered kept them from starving. Requisition parties took everything else. First ones came by talking all high about the struggles of the Confederacy and brave boys fighting here and there, and they handed Miss' Emily more of the money that wouldn't buy anything, or chitties worth even less. The officers made lists and tallied up figures, but all of them stole when they weren't watched. Dundee had tried to talk to Miss' Emily about it, but she was already sunk down and wouldn't deny them. Later on, when the rougher men came, they just made an excuse or two and took what was left.

A time after Mr. Walker went into the house, a good time after, Miss' Emily screamed. She screamed, *"No!"* Over and over again. Then she set to cursing in words she had not even used on Marse George over his doings in Charleston and the rottenness he put in her and the child. It shocked Dundee, who had not heard her raise her voice all the year and longer. He didn't think there was that much caring about anything left in her.

He went on with his scrubbing, though. Because it wasn't a hitting-and-hurting scream. It was just a feel-hurt kind of cry, loud and pained as it was. A bad-news-just-spoke cry. Although she had not sounded anything like that when word came about Marse George or even her brothers.

Miss' Emily's voice turned raw and crumpled. Mr. Walker stepped around the house and into the working yard. He had on the look of a man who wants to go off as soon as he can, but he headed over to Dundee. Straight over.

"Dundee," he said.

Dundee backed out of the pen and straightened up.

"I like to see a fellow who isn't too proud to work," Mr. Walker said. He was a clean-made man who had not gone off to war with the others. "Fellow who doesn't need barking at to get him going. Black, white, or in-between somewheres, I just like a fellow who has the sense to work."

"Yes, sir," Dundee said, in the voice he had learned to use to say nothing at all.

"Look here," Mr. Walker said. "Things are going to start going your way. I've been watching you. Know all about you. Got sense enough to keep your niggers reined in. Fellow like you is going to make something of himself, this war is over. You want to make something out of yourself, don't you?"

"I just do what seems right," Dundee said carefully.

"Well, the right thing for you to do is keep the rest of them coloreds from running off. There's going to be big changes around here, I can tell you. Things are going to look up for every one of them. Every last one. Come next growing season, they're even going to have jingle money in their pockets. You tell them that. But don't let them run off."

"Ain't nobody running off," Dundee said. "It's a bad time."

"That's right! But it's going to be a real good time for a fellow who has him some sense. Who isn't afraid to work hard. A fellow his people will listen to."

"Yes, sir."

"Look here. Miss' Emily and the girl are going away soon. To someplace where they'll be looked after." Mr. Walker made a face like a man who had just crawled around in an outhouse in high summer. "Nobody can live like that. In that filth. It isn't decent. I'm ashamed of myself for not doing something sooner."

"Yes, sir." Dundee looked at the stick-pin in the visitor's cravat, not at his eyes. He had seen all he needed to of the man's eyes in half a minute. Maybe less.

"And the things people are saying," Mr. Walker continued. "About that partisan ranger fellow, Clarke. And his men. The things people say about what's been going on up here nights. It isn't decent. They should be horsewhipped."

Dundee tensed, though not to notice. There were some things he didn't want to hear from a white man's lips. Some things it didn't pay to know from a white man, even if you already knew them from elsewheres.

"Well, I've taken action," Mr. Walker went on. "Yes, I have. Miss' Emily and that girl are going to be looked after, so don't you all go worrying about them. And I'm going to see that you people are all looked after, too. Hear me?"

"Yes, sir."

"You all have something to eat? You all have Christmas dinner fixings?" He smiled. "You're a smart nigger. I bet you've got hams and sausage and everything under the sun hid out somewheres. So no white-trash Confederates, nor even a Yankee could find it. You all have your Christmas dinner for tomorrow?"

"Yes, sir," Dundee said. "We don't lack for nothing. Thank you kindly." It wasn't true, not strictly. There'd be eating, but nothing fond. Just what a man could live on. Just what could fill a child's belly. But Dundee didn't want to take from this man. And he knew the man didn't really want to give. He told himself it was mean and selfish of him, that he was obliged to take what he could to feed folks up. Anybody else would take with both hands, say thank you, and maybe they would be right. But Dundee just didn't want to take from this man. Or from any other, tell the truth. But especially not from this one.

"I admire that, too. Not greedy. I hate a grabbing man," Mr. Walker said. "White or black. No, a fellow like you is going to make something of himself in the days to come. Now that the law's on the way back. The good old U.S. Constitution." He looked at Dundee so hard it forced his eyes up. Mr. Walker had brown eyes, the kind that fooled you into thinking there was a softness there, if you didn't know better.

"I always was a staunch supporter of the Union," Mr. Walker went on. "You know that, don't you? Oh, I couldn't say anything much. Not with folks all heated up about the war. Damned fool business. I never was for it. I was always a Union man, but I had to watch my step. But I always supported the Union. I bet you knew that, didn't you? I bet you could tell."

"Like you say, sir," Dundee told him.

"That's right. And you make sure all your other coloreds know it, anybody asks. 'Mr. Howard Walker was always a good Union man.' That's all they need to say about it, no need to confuse them with more than that. No, the law's coming back, and freedom for all you folks. Emancipation. We're going to see us a bright, new day."

"Yes, sir."

Mr. Walker resettled his hat like a man thinking about moving on. "And you don't let any of your people get all upset when they come for Miss' Emily and the girl. It's for their own good. You tell your people that. And I'm going to see to it that everybody lives good, afterward. You tell them that, too."

"Yes, sir."

The visitor began to turn away, but paused and thrust a tangle of fingers into his waistcoat pocket. He held out a ten-cent piece.

"Here's a Christmas gift for you, Dundee. Going to be the first of many."

WHEN THE BUGGY rode off, Dundee tossed the coin into the mud. Let somebody find it. That was all right. But he wasn't going to take it. He knew that was the sin of pride in him. And Honeymine would have got her temper up to see it. But he just wasn't going to take it.

That evening, he called everyone together back of the quarters and did what preaching he could manage, now that the reverend was gone. He wasn't satisfied. But wasn't anybody else going to do it better. Or do it at all. So he spoke as best he could about the Baby Jesus and how he was born in a hay trough for cows and donkeys and didn't even have a shuck mattress, but rose up anyway. Because the Lord, who made Heaven and Earth, had a mind that way. The Lord could make the lame to walk, and the blind to see, and he put his power into the Baby Jesus, so folks could hope on him. Then they sang. And after they settled, the time came to talk and they all gathered around close in the cold, close to each other but not to Dundee. They always cleaved him a spot of his own. Even Honeymine did, if it was a meeting.

"Going to be a Christmas gif' this year?" Old Pull asked.

Other voices started in to talking the same nonsense, though they all knew better.

"Ain't no Christmas gift coming," Dundee told them. "And ain't one of you figured any different. So don't go fool talking. You're lucky them rangers didn't dig up what little food we got. You can all be thankful to the Lord there'll be biscuits in your bellies come tomorrow."

But he could remember the better days, the honey times of Christmas, when most hearts eased. Even Marse George had been openhanded that one day of the year, so long as his luck was running fair. Days when folks lined up at the back porch and took their turn stepping in to say their "Merry Christmas" and get a hand-me-down dress or maybe a bolt of cloth, an old suitcoat and shoes that would hold together for another year. And there was plenty to eat, say that much. Sometimes even a little buying money to spend with the peddler man.

Later, Marse George would come down to the quarters himself, to seek out Dundee, who had stopped lining up at the porch years back, after the trouble that brought the Connelly brothers out from town to bind him up and give him a whipping Marse George was too faint a man to give by his own hand. Marse George would come on down to the quarters under that cold winter sun with a package under one arm and a big jug of poor-white whisky under the other. Always had that behind-the-skin look of shame on his face, that old shame that wouldn't quit, though Marse George always stepped through the door grinning. The package would hold an outfit of clothes for Dundee, store-bought to fit a bigger man than Marse George's hand-me-downs would suit, and he would put down the whisky by the door, giving the charge of it to Dundee who didn't drink anymore, not since his Salvation, saying, "Make sure they don't do nothing crazy, Dundee. I'm counting on you to keep them from getting all drunk and crazy, hear?"

"Listen," Dundee said to the flock gathered around him in the chill. "There's going to be changes. Place is going to run proper again, come spring. Everything's going to be all right."

"What you talking, Dundee?"

"Miss' Emily and the child are going off. Mr. Walker's going to see to them. He's going to have the say around here, looks like."

"Bankman Walker? Say he even treats white folks like they black."

"We're free now," Hector said. "Ain't nobody going to have no more say. We been set free."

"Well, you might be free," Dundee told him, "but food ain't. You want to go, go on. I ain't going to stop any man wants to go. But just ask yourself where tomorrow's dinner going to come from."

"That Bankman Walker," Old Pull said. "I don't know."

"Everything's going to be all right," Dundee repeated, firmly. And he saw the years remaining to him, whether many or few, in a new bondage to the people gathered around him that Christmas Eve. In this Babylon, this Egypt. Truth was he wanted to go. Go anywhere else. Take Honeymine and just go. But he was the shepherd. He understood that, as surely as if the finger of the Lord had touched him.

These people were his flock, and his burden and his trial, helpless because they chose to be, which he could not understand. Helpless because it was easy enough to be that way. Waiting to be told. All his lifetime, Dundee had been told, and he did not like it. He would start a task before dawn, if he knew it needed to be done, just to avoid being told to do it. But folks were different. There were folks needed to be told to put the food in their mouths and chew it. Maybe someday it would be different. But he didn't expect he would live to see it.

He wanted them to just get *up*. To stand up and do for themselves. But the doing sorts had run off early. These here were the least in the Kingdom. Without him, they would surely stray. And there would be a crying and a lamentation in the land.

He was an intelligent man. He knew that. He saw with clear eyes. And he could see enough of the day after next to know that he was faced off with a long struggle against this Mr. Walker and all the hosts of lesser devils like him. A struggle to feed his sheep. To keep them from all harm.

"You all go back now," he said. "It's cold."

But he could not let them go into the holy night with such a sorrow over them.

"Next year," Dundee cried, taking them by surprise. "Next year there's going to be a Christmas gift. For everybody. I promise."

HE PRAYED THAT night for the Lord to guide him, to take his hand and lead him. To tell him what was right and how to do. But Heaven was quiet. So he just said his thanks and pulled Honeymine to him, her complaining how he was worse than a bear and how was she supposed to sleep like that? But that was what she always said, and she settled warmly to him, comfortable and easy with the years, and maybe that was all the blessing a man could ask.

In the morning he woke to the smell of ham. It opened his eyes. The smell was rich as the private things between a man and a woman. Frying ham. The smell was thick as stirred-up dust.

"What's that there, woman?" he asked.

"You know what that is. You know perfectly well."

"Where'd you come by that, now?"

"If you don't ask, I won't tell. Get up, now. Get up and get your Christmas breakfast."

He got up. And went out in the chill of the morning to take care of what needed to be taken care of. Then he cleaned his hands and splashed his face with water and went back in.

Smelled like Heaven must. Good ham. Biscuits, Honeymine's biscuits, and weren't none better. Even eggs.

"You been out stealing, woman? Eggs, too?"

She faced him, hot-faced from the fire. "When I ever steal a thing? When I ever? I was a good Christian woman before you was ever a Christian man. Talk to me like that."

He saw the ham then. Not the frying-up ham, but the rest of it. If it wasn't a miracle, it was a glory.

"Sit down there, Dundee. You sit down there and let me do."

He sat down. She served him first, served him a bounty, then sat down across the board table from him with a helping of her own.

"Merry Christmas," she told him. "And first off, you're going to say me some nice Christian words."

He did. Best he could. And they began to eat.

"Bless you, woman," he said, with the inside of his mouth richer than it had been in a year, maybe longer. "You're my Christmas gift every day of the year."

"What did that Bankman Walker say to you yesterday?"

"Not much."

"You tell me now. You got me to worrying. You tell me just what he said." She reached her hands to take his plate away from him, but stopped shy.

"Said times going to get better. Specially for me."

"You believe that man?"

"No."

"What you going to do?"

"Nothing. Nothing just now. Wait and see."

He saw that her eyes were troubled.

"It's going to be all right," he told her. "Maybe things will turn better. Couldn't be much worse."

"That's no comfort. That's no comfort to me at all. What else he say to you."

He grinned through a biscuit sop of egg. "Said he was always a good Union man. Said how he was always a Yankee lover. Thought I was listening to Mr. Lincoln himself."

Honeymine rolled her eyes. He felt her coming back to him again. "I remember him was yelling how the Yankees going to free the coloreds and set them up high above the white folks and how they all had to fight to the death."

"I guess some of them took him at his word. Marse George, anyhow."

"What else he say? You want more coffee?"

"Said how they going to come and take Miss' Emily and that Polly off. Treat them decent."

And then he paused, with a pink strip of ham halfway to his mouth. Something moved inside him. Down deep. The kind of thing you don't want to have moving around, the way it shakes you. Something swells up sad and lonely inside you, and you see yourself different, and you see the world different and maybe new. And maybe the world looks better, but you don't.

"Fix me a plate, woman."

"You ain't done with that one."

"Fix me up a plate. A full one. That big plate there, tin one. Fill it all up."

She drew back and her eyes spoiled on him. "What for? Who you want that plate for?"

"I'm going to take it up to the high house. You know they sitting there with nothing to eat. Christmas morning."

"No!" she said. "No, I ain't feeding them no more! Not with what all I had to do to raise this. I done all this for you, Dundee. Not for her."

"Honeymine . . ."

"Don't you do that. Take your hands away from me." Then she looked up at him. "Not for her. Not after all been done to me. And all been done to you."

He looked at her. And he understood her. He even knew that she was right, as far as the justice of this world went.

"We're free now, Dundee. You don't have to go bowing down to her or anybody no more. That crazy woman. She was colored, they'd lock her in a cellar. And that child ain't been washed in a year. There's calves smarter than that child, with more sense. Let them be, Dundee. After all they done to us. Just you let them be."

"Woman . . ."

"Please. I'm asking you now." Folding in of a sudden. Meek.

Anger in a man burns for years. Won't burn up like firewood. Anger lasts, and maybe that's the eternal hellfire of Damnation. Maybe that right there. Maybe it wasn't just anger, but something worse. The meanness that makes a man want to hide his face from God. More than meanness, too. Say the word to yourself, now. The hatred.

But when he spoke, Dundee did not speak in anger. Not so you could tell, if you didn't know him deep. His voice never got to making too much noise. Something in that voice, though. Something that told you to go careful, not to strike no match.

"I won't," he said, "be low as them. Don't you see that, woman? Be low as them, it lets them hold to all the things they're onto believing, everything they say about high and low, white folks and colored, all them wicked things." He looked down at the bounty her love had set before him, knowing well enough that it was only the smallest part of the bounty her love had brought him. "Think it sits easy with me? To fight down what I got burning in my heart? But I *won't* be low as them, I swear it. I won't be low as them."

He could not even look at her for remembering. A remembering that was like a sickness, that chewed on a man until there was nothing left but hatred and bones. "Day word came how that man got himself killed, my heart leapt up. I felt *joy*, woman. I wanted to get up and shout it. And when it was first spoke clear how that child wasn't right, and wasn't going to be right anytime soon, it pleased me. I told myself it was a judgement. For what that woman done to you. And after all he done."

Dundee looked down, not at the plate, but right through the table and the floor and the earth itself. "When they started saying how everything was going to a poorness around here, how everything was gambled away and squandered and never coming back, how that man wasn't good for nothing, it pleased me. And I just worked the harder for it, and drove folks to work like they wasn't used to working, 'cause, Lord, I was going to show them all how I could make a bad field sprout money when that . . . that *man* couldn't make the best one pay up five cent." He paused, as if catching his breath after hard labor. "All the while, I called myself a Christian. All the while. Other day, even, when I went into that house, saw it all broke up. And them two nothing but husks, not folks at all, curled up in their own smells, in their own foulness, how it says. Even then, my heart was pleased. To see them fallen. To see them . . ."

He looked up then, looking at the woman he loved, the woman who loved him, looking past the permanent welt set down across her face by Miss' Emily's hand, past all that. "Maybe you know," he said. "I can't tell. Maybe you do. But I have held hatred in my heart. Hatred like a worm down in my heart. Swelling up and growing 'til it chokes me. And now I just want it out of me. Can't you see that? How I just want to stop hating them? Even for a day? How they ain't even worth the hating no more?"

Honeymine was crying, but he couldn't tell how that crying was.

"They done the worst thing to me," he told her. "Making me hate them like that. Preacher always said they could rule over our bodies, but not our souls. And I went and let them rule over my soul, too. Served it up to them like a damned fool. Gave them that gift, when they didn't even ask for it and had no need for it at all. Gave them my immortal soul." His body, the hand upon the table, felt heavy as a wagon full of sacks. "And I ain't going to do it no more. I won't be low as them."

"They took what should of been yours," Honeymine said, in a whisper. "He ruined me for you." Talking most to herself, way women do.

Dundee was all spoke out. Heavy and empty at the same time. No lack of talking in this world. What a man does is what matters. "You go over there to that cupboard," he told the companion of his life and heart. "Get that Holy Bible down. And sit right here when you come back. You just do that, and don't deny me."

She did what he asked.

"Read me the part. Part in Matthew."

"What part?"

"The Baby Jesus part, woman. What day you think this is?"

And she read to him, and he listened, without touching the wonders left on his plate. He listened to her read, watching her finger trace the lines on the speckled pages. After that, he closed his eyes and listened.

"See now," he said when she had finished.

Honeymine didn't answer. She was done crying, though.

"See now," he began again. "If those wise men over there could travel all that way and kneel down and offer unto Him gifts, if they could kneel down like that before a little baby, I figure I can carry a plate up to the high house for Miss' Emily and the child."

"You're too heart-soft," she said. But she was already up to her feet and doing. "You're too heart-soft, and that's the truth. You'd give away your right hand, somebody asked you for it. But I suppose I could've picked worse cotton."

"I picked you, woman. Just remember. I picked you."

DUNDEE CARRIED THE big plate up to the house with a piece of muslin spread to keep things warm. Wasn't no smoke coming from the main chimney or any of the others. He saw that. And it was cold.

He went in the back porch door and two field mice ran out past him. Everything seemed broke down just the same as before, nothing shifted or fixed up at all. Same smell to make you sick. Miss' Emily was in the visiting parlor again, though Polly was in her lap now, great big child that she was.

The room was freezing cold.

Dundee turned a table rightside-up and set the plate on it. The girl was already stirring. Couldn't talk, and she must of been ten, at least ten. But she could smell the way a dog does. She sat right up and watched him lift off the rag.

The girl started out of her mother's lap, but Miss' Emily caught her and pulled her back against her, holding on tight, though the girl put up a little fight then fell to crying.

"We don't need your charity," Miss' Emily said suddenly. "My father was Senator Darnell. We don't need any charity from you. You'll see."

"Yes, ma'am. I figure that's true," Dundee said. He had bent to start the fireplace going again. He knew she wouldn't let the child eat, or eat herself, 'til he was gone. But they had to have them a fire. Cold enough to freeze water in that room.

"You just take that plate back out of here," she said, in a voice hollow as an empty barrel. A voice all sick inside.

"I can't do that now, Miss' Emily. You know how Honey-mine is. She sent this Christmas eating up here for you, and I wouldn't get no peace if I tried to take it back. I'll just leave it here and you can throw it out, if you want. But I'm just going to leave it here."

He felt the fire's first hint of warm. Room had to be cold for a man to feel such a little flicker like that make a difference to his hands. He fed more splinters in between the logs, wanting to be sure the fire took before he left them.

The child sat on its mother's lap, whimpering. Miss' Emily hardly seemed to see Dundee now. Didn't see him at all any-more.

"Come to this," she whispered. "Now I've come to this."

Dundee left them like that, with the fire growing and the food still holding warm on the table. Soon as he got down the hall a ways, he heard the girl run across the room and strike the table with her shriveled-up body and stop there. Then he heard a woman's unsteady footsteps, and sobbing after.

"Merry Christmas, now," Dundee said, although he was too far away to be heard any longer. You did what you thought was right, what you thought the Lord would want. Sometimes it took, and sometimes it didn't. But you kept trying.

He stepped outside into the cold air and the quiet light of Christmas, then turned his steps toward the rest of his days.

A Christmas Request to the Reader

The stories that are set down here
Are meant to heighten Christmas cheer,
While hinting, in their humble way,
At what we owe this holy-day.

So, when you close this little book,
Pause a moment, just to look
At each of those who bless your life,
Friend or child, man or wife.

If they have failed you, please forgive,
As He forgave, so we might live.
Lay aside your mortal pride,
And try to see how they have tried.

Then open up your heart and call
A "Merry Christmas!" to them all.

—OWEN PARRY

FIC
PAR

Parry, Owen.

Our simple gifts.

$14.95

33910010526706
01/03/2003

DATE			
		DISCARDED